PAWS, PROMISES, AND PERIL

WHISKEY MYSTERY #4

In Your Face Ink LLC
9524 W. Camelback Road
#130-182
Glendale, AZ 85305
www.inyourfaceink.com
www.whiskeydogmysteries.com

First printed in the United States of America by In Your Face Ink LLC

ISBN: 979-8-9924943-0-3 (hardback)
ISBN: 979-8-9924943-1-0 (paperback)
ISBN: 979-8-9924943-2-7 (e-book)

Book design and cover by Rick Schank of Purple Couch Creative

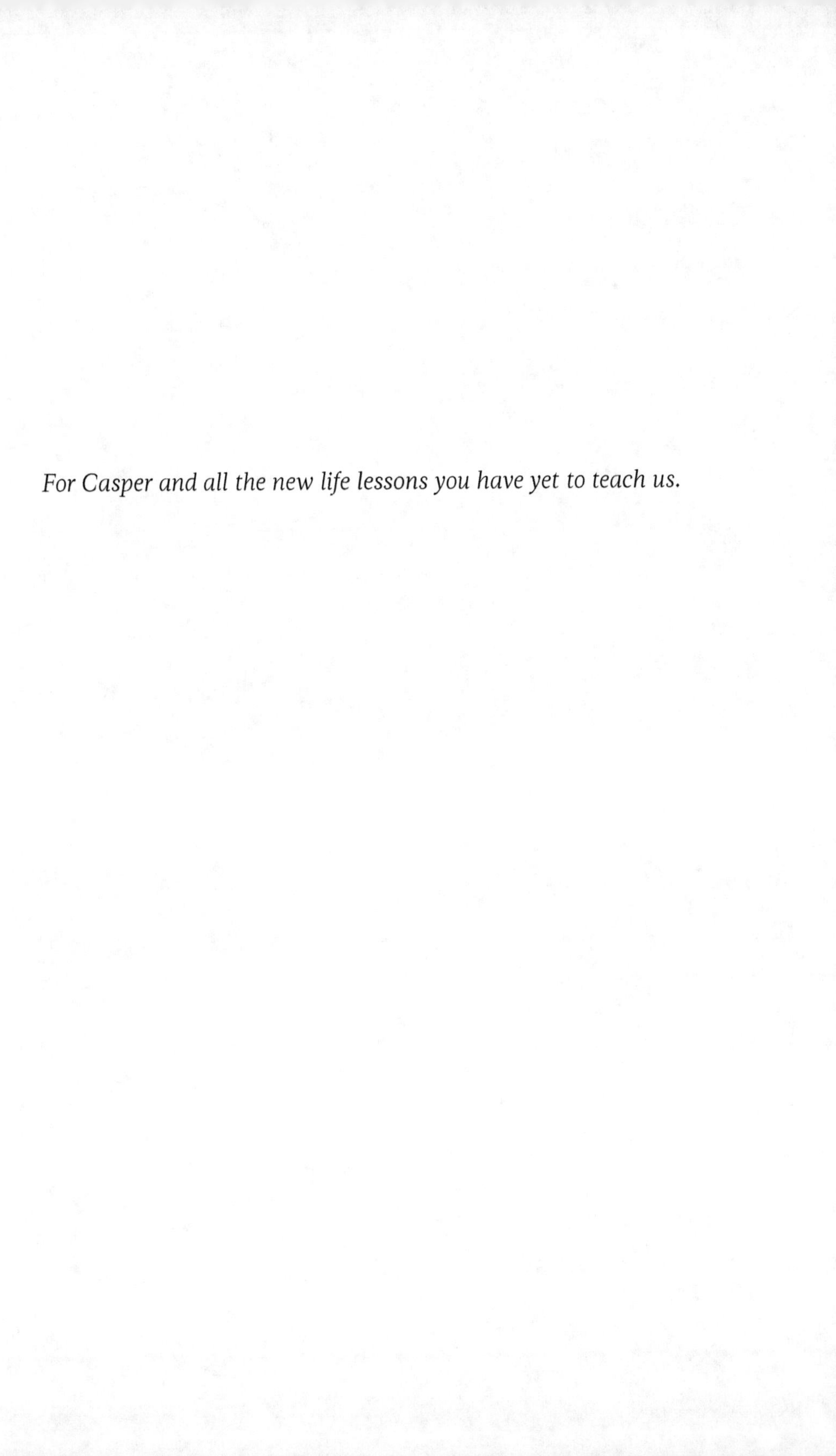

For Casper and all the new life lessons you have yet to teach us.

PARADE OF INFORMATION

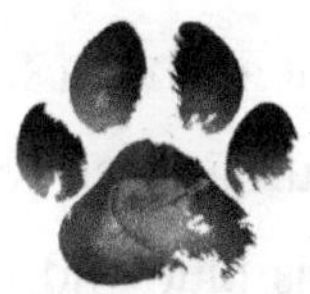

CHAPTER ONE

"**W**hy did I ever decide to oversee the annual Valentine's Day Pet Parade and festivities?" Sarah Carter asked herself for the hundredth time. Sure, it had seemed like a fun idea last month when a canine in a cupid costume crossed her social media feed and caused her and her assistant, Emily Colt, to chuckle and wish that their town had a parade of pets. But now that the event was fourteen days away, and her grooming salon, Carter's Canine Coiffure, was slammed with appointments before the big day—plus she was still navigating the permits, vendors, and logistics not to mention the pet parents who demanded more attention and control than the worst bridezillas—Sarah wondered if her amusing brainstorm with Em was turning into a nightmare.

Cottageville, a small town in Iowa, had its share of characters and animal lovers, or maybe the animal obsessed was more like it. The parade was turning into a huge to-do, with more than one hundred pets registered to march. And it wasn't only the pawed and canine variety. Em's friend Taylor signed up Iggy the iguana to crawl down Main Street. Five people planned to walk cats on leashes—which with some cats was as effective as trying to herd them. Pat from Cottageville Animal Rescue was bringing a whole menagerie for which she needed to find foster and permanent homes, including a bow-wearing descented skunk named Petunia. And just yesterday, Sarah received a call from a guy asking if his blue and red tarantula could take part in the parade. She wasn't sure how any of this would work out. Even her Australian red heeler cattle dog, Whiskey, who loved almost every human and most critters, was suspicious of the skunk, and she had no idea how he'd respond to an arachnid.

And when you combined the wearing of costumes—which triggered reluctance and feelings of insecurity in some of furred and feathered set—with species who have been stereotyped sworn enemies for a reason, those cats and dogs, rabbits and skunks, snakes and spiders, hamsters and guinea pigs, and the lizard or two, could cause things to go very wrong very quickly. If one animal felt threatened or a lack of confidence, chaos could ensue.

Sarah felt her heart rate increase and her anxiety spike just thinking about it. She intentionally took some deep cleansing breaths and sighed them out, willing in some calm and inner wisdom. She told herself, "You've got this," but the words sounded hollow, even in her head. Instead, she focused on what was in front of her: the park and its expansive sparkling ice crystal designs. She gazed at the top bar of the swing set and the side of the slides, which sported icicle drips. Mandala patterns bloomed in ice lace between the climbing ropes on the north end of the jungle gym. Winter bloomed in all of her beauty, with Mother Nature as artist extraordinaire.

Sarah zipped her navy-blue puffy jacket to ward off the February chill and scrunched her neck into the jacket's collar, like a turtle shrinking into its shell. She should have put a knit beanie on top of her damp auburn hair before she left the house. But she was in a hurry. On days like this, when the wind was whipping, she envied Whiskey, with his double coat of fur. He was off-leash as usual and ahead of her, following his nose along the dusting of snow gracing the grass like powdered sugar atop a chocolate crinkle cookie. The park was empty at six-thirty on a weekday, which was the way Sarah liked it since it was usually her thinking time. But right now, thinking was the last thing she needed to do.

So, she watched Whiskey on his sniff fest and wondered what had been through the park before them. A raccoon or opossum, possibly? Or had it been one of his friends, like Sascha the German shepherd and his human, police chief James Order? Whiskey's interest seemed intrigued, not agitated, as he followed a trail invisible to Sarah's eyes. He eventually led her out of the park and to the front porch of Bill, an elderly widower who was popular with the gray-haired grannies, and who sat outside with his morning coffee and newspaper every day of the year, regardless of the temperature. Next to Bill was the target of Whiskey's mission to visit: a gallon jar of dog treats.

"Top of the morning to you, Whiskey, Sarah," Bill greeted, reaching into the jar of treats. He wore a trapper hat with the flaps up, an old quilted flannel jacket buttoned over what looked to Sarah like a gray sweatshirt and jeans that may have been flannel lined, and wintry sheep's fleece-lined slippers over his socks. He asked Whiskey to slap him five, and once the dog's right paw hit Bill's palm, he handed Whiskey the biscuit. "How are you today?" Bill's eyes met Sarah's.

"I'm okay. Stressing a little over the parade and Valentine's Day festivities," she admitted.

"The guys at the hall asked if you needed help with security or route set-up, check-in, or anything else. We're available the day of or to help with anything you need before or after, including clean-up." Though Bill had never been a farmer, he had joined the Grange Hall years ago for companionship after his wife had died.

"Wow. That's so generous of you. I would love some help. I think Janice Jenkins said she'd work the check-in table, but she could probably use an assistant and I could use help with set-up, security, and clean-up, for sure. Do you want me to create a sign-up sheet for you to take to the hall, or should anyone who wants to volunteer just contact me?" Janice Jenkins lived across the street from Sarah, and she and Bill were close friends, maybe more.

"You have enough on your plate, Sarah. I can be the point person and coordinate all of the positions and people. Just let me know what jobs you need to have filled. I'm happy to help and have plenty of time." Bill took a sip of his coffee.

"I can't thank you enough." Sarah leaned down and gave him a side hug. "I'll send you an e-mail with the details. Come on, Whiskey, we've got to get going. Thanks again, Bill."

Sarah took off at a jog back through the still-empty park, with Whiskey running alongside her. The overwhelm she had been feeling for days had been carried away like a helium balloon, thanks to Bill and his Grange Hall friends.

When they returned to the craftsman bungalow that Sarah had inherited almost seven years before from her grandmother, Gigi, she fed Whiskey his breakfast, which he gobbled down in what seemed like a breath. Then, before she forgot, Sarah pulled out the folder for the pet parade and typed up the email to Bill on the various volunteer positions that needed to be assigned. She reiterated how grateful she was for their willingness to help. And she offered to take Bill out to dinner to thank him once the festivities were over.

Sarah grabbed her to-go tumbler, slid her feet into boots and her arms into the sleeves of her jacket. She added her scarf and beanie to the ensemble this time, before she zipped her jacket, and then she and Whiskey locked the door to their home and walked back toward the park to go to work. As they approached the children's playground, Sarah spotted Gigi's best friend and the woman who had become an adopted grandmother to her, Gladys Rossmiller, and her miniature poodles, Kahlo and Cassatt, who were sniffing below the swings. Gladys was wrapped in a long royal blue coat, with a lavender scarf wrapped and wrapped and wrapped around her eighty-year-old neck. She wore matching knit gloves and a lavender knit hat with a daisy at its crown. Sarah thought she looked adorable and fashionable as a former art teacher and painter should. Whiskey ran to romp with the poodles.

"Good morning, Sarah," Gladys called. "Brisk today."

"Hi, Gladys." Sarah gave her a hug. "It is a bit chilly, but at least the sun is shining."

"Always a glorious day when it's sunny. Did you get the registration for my girls? I found them the cutest outfits. I got Kahlo a beret and sweater. Both have a white background with red hearts. And for Cassatt I found a kissing booth head piece."

"Oh my. I can't wait to see them. Those sound perfect."

"Did you find Whiskey a costume yet?"

"He's not big on costumes. He doesn't like to wear coats or sweaters either. I think the best I can expect is for him to wear a red velvet bow tie on his collar."

"He's handsome as is, but that would make him debonair." Gladys reached a gloved hand to stroke Whiskey's head. He smiled up at her, like he understood what she said, his fluffy red and white-tipped tail swishing like a single windshield wiper, scattering the dusting of snow. Gladys continued, "I know, dear, you need to be on your way to make it to work on time. Thank you for stopping to say hello." And then to her poodles, she said, "Come on, girls, let's do your business so we can go back to the house and get warm."

Sarah kissed Gladys' cold cheek. "I'll come by this weekend for some tea and a chat."

"That would be lovely."

"I'll race you to the park entrance, Whiskey." Sarah jogged as she said the words, and Whiskey blew past her, his tongue hanging out, like "nah nah nah nah, You can't catch me."

Sarah chuckled and picked up speed, but she couldn't keep up with his four-legged gallop.

Whiskey sat and waited for her at the edge of Main Street, and then when Cottageville's only light turned green for their direction, they walked across the road and down a block to Java and Juice. Sarah opened the painted cherry door, and the bell chimed overhead. Whiskey walked into the café ahead of her, his head held high, and went straight to the counter as no one was in line. One of his favorite humans and Sarah's boyfriend, Jared Greene, was behind the register. He gave Whiskey a homemade chicken biscuit after making him shake for it.

"Mi'lady." Jared acknowledged Sarah by bowing, in a silly shtick they had done since they first met years ago, but that had become more infrequent since they had become a couple in December.

"My lord." Sarah curtsied, holding out an imaginary skirt, and then handed him her tumbler, which he filled with black dark roast coffee, before passing it back to her. Sarah was surprised to see the café mostly empty. Two people Sarah didn't know, a middle aged man and an older woman, sat at one table near the bathroom. They looked deep in conversation.

Café owner Ginger Jones came from Java and Juice's backroom, her arms ladened with trays of pastries. Her blond curls were pulled into a high ponytail, and she wore a charcoal thermal shirt beneath denim overalls, which were cuffed at the ankles above gray suede booties. "Hey, bestie," Ginger greeted Sarah. "I think you and Em need to try these." Ginger nodded her head toward the tray of scones that looked like they were liberally dotted with candy cinnamon hearts and dark chocolate chunks. "And I tried a new salad recipe today. Ginger beef with carrots, purple onions, greens, and udon noodles, so get that for lunch."

"What she said," Sarah said to Jared.

He took two scones from the tray Ginger set on the counter, before she bent to slide open the doors to the glass case so she could refill it. And then he turned to the cooler and picked up two salads and put those in the bag and then the scones on top. He threw in an extra biscuit for Whiskey for later, too. "May I make you supper tonight?" Jared asked as Sarah used her card to pay.

"I'd never say no to that." Sarah leaned across the counter and pressed her lips against his. "Come on, Whisk. We'll see Jared later. Bye, Ginger. I love you."

By the time Sarah arrived at Carter's Canine Coiffure, her assistant had already opened the business for the day and had Whiskey's pal, seventy-five pounds of power Spike the pit bull, in the tub.

"Hey, Em," Sarah said, upon opening the green door of the Coiffure. She stopped short when she spied Daniel Snyder, owner of Buck and Son Hardware and Ginger's boyfriend, standing in the waiting room. The sight surprised Sarah, as Daniel and Ginger lived with no pets. "Hey, Daniel." Whiskey walked up to Daniel demanding some attention.

Daniel leaned down to scratch the dog's ears before standing upright again. "Sarah, I hope this is an okay time. I figured I'd catch you before you got too busy." He shifted his weight from his right foot to his left, but his eyes, golden brown the same color as Whiskey's, sought hers.

Sarah thought he looked more nervous than usual. "Let me put this bag down and take off my coat and I'll be right with you." Sarah put the salads in the fridge and the scones on the table in the back. She took off her winter wrappings and donned her denim dog print apron and then returned to the waiting area, which was where the living room was when the building was someone's home.

Sarah remained standing since Daniel hadn't sat on the sofas. "So, what's up?" Sarah's green eyes bore into his.

"I need your help. Planning a surprise. For Ginger." His speech was more choppy than normal.

"Oh?" Sarah raised her eyebrows.

"I'm going... to ask her to marry me. But I need your help."

Sarah was squealing inside but trying to keep her cool. "Of course. Anything, Daniel. I'm so happy for both of you." She grabbed his forearm and squeezed. All of Cottageville knew the story as Daniel was a lifelong local: Daniel had married his high school sweetheart and had taken over the family's hardware store from his father while she worked as a paralegal at her father's law firm. They were overjoyed when they found out they were expecting a baby. Only, partway through the pregnancy, Daniel's wife hemorrhaged, and at the end of a workday, he found her collapsed in a puddle of blood on the kitchen floor. Both his unborn child and the love of his life were gone.

Years had gone by as he lived with the grief and went through the motions of life. But then last year, he asked Ginger, whom he had known since childhood, out on a date to a picnic next to a creek way outside of town. That one secretive date (so the whole town wouldn't know their business before they knew what they wanted) led to two and then to many, before Daniel sold the house he and his wife had lived in, and he and Ginger purchased an old farmhouse that they had been slowly remodeling, as they did much of the work themselves.

And though Ginger had confided in Sarah that she didn't care if they ever got married—especially if it would trigger trauma for Daniel—apparently, he felt differently. He was ready to pop the question and Sarah was sure Ginger would say yes. But what did he have in mind?

CHAPTER TWO

"How can I help? What do you need me to do?"

Before Daniel could answer, the green door of the Coiffure opened and Whiskey trotted the few steps to meet their new guests. Wearing a full-length soft cashmere black coat open in the front and black knee-high, heeled boots and carrying Pierre, her buff-color French bulldog, Daphne Smith was the height of French fashion, though she had never been outside of Cottageville. "*Bonjour,* Sarah. *Bonjour,* Whiskey. *Enchanté,* Daniel." She pronounced Daniel's name like her American townspeople pronounced the female version of the name *Danielle,* with the accent on the second syllable.

"*Bonjour,* Daphne," Sarah and Daniel said in unison, which

made them both chuckle.

Daphne surprised Sarah when she set Pierre on the counter and proceeded, in English, to explain that her baby was experiencing both dermatitis and a bit of lip-fold pyoderma so she asked if Sarah could bathe him in a medicated shampoo. Sarah fingered the folds under Pierre's chin to inspect the severity of the pyoderma.

Daniel cringed at the small screaming red sores under Pierre's mouth and said, "I'll call you later, Sarah," before he headed out the door.

"Looking forward to it," Sarah called after him. To Daphne, Sarah asked, "Is Pierre on an antibiotic? I have a medicated shampoo with benzoyl peroxide we can use."

"*Oui, le shampoing est parfait,*" Daphne replied.

"Okay," Sarah said. "We'll see you in two hours. How long has he been taking the antibiotic?"

"*Quinze jours.*"

Two weeks meant Pierre was either two-thirds or half way through the prescription. She wondered how bad it looked before because the smattering of lesions were still fairly inflamed. "How you doing, buddy?" she asked as she held Pierre to her chest and opened the counter at its hinge and walked through.

Emily had Spike on the stainless steel table with his head in the leather strap and she was blowing him dry while running a brush along his back. Whiskey went to assist Emily by standing on his hind legs and putting his front paws on the steel table top. Spike's eyes rolled downward and he gave one sharp bark acknowledging his buddy was back at his side.

Sarah held Pierre under her arm like a football as she searched on a shelf for the special shampoo. When she found it, she carried the bottle and the bulldog to the wash tub. "Here you go, love," Sarah said as she set the dog on the bottom of the basin. She turned the water to lukewarm and then sprayed the dog all over before turning the water off and pouring a quarter-size dollop of shampoo into her hand. She worked into his fur with her fingers, giving Pierre a gentle massage that he seemed to appreciate since he leaned into her hands and closed his eyes. Sarah ensured the shampoo got into his armpits and leg creases, as well as all over his belly as she massaged his muscles for the ten minutes it took the shampoo to be effective.

Once she was satisfied enough time had passed, she rinsed him all over until the water ran clear. Then she wrapped him in a fluffy towel so that only his face showed. As she carried him to a grooming table, she asked Emily, "Did Tony say he and Spike were marching in the pet parade? I don't remember seeing their registration."

"He didn't say." Em wiped her hands on her apron before pulling the scone Sarah had bought her out of the bag and taking a big bite. She audibly released a "Mmmm" as she chewed. After she swallowed she said, "Thanks for this. It's a decadent party in my mouth."

"The cinnamon hearts are like a burst of passion and the dark chocolate is like a soulful conversation. Together, it's the best love story in one scone." Sarah grinned.

"Aren't you a poet. You should tell that to Ginger. She could use it in her advertising."

Emily took another bite.

Sarah glanced over at Whiskey and Spike while she patted the towel against Pierre.

Spike and Whiskey were playing and wrestling over a big stuffed alligator in the front room. Their tails wagged furiously as they tugged the alligator back and forth, growling in jest. Spike, the larger of the two, had the advantage of size, but Whiskey was quick and clever, darting around to gain better leverage. The stuffed alligator squeaked loudly as they tussled, filling the room with a mix of chaos and excitement.

Suddenly, Whiskey let go, causing Spike to tumble backward with the alligator clutched like a prized trophy in his jaws. Whiskey barked and pounced again, ready for round two.

"They have so much fun," Emily said, placing the last bite of scone in her mouth.

"Indeed." Sarah finished towel-drying Pierre since she knew the heat of the blow dryer could further inflame his skin. Once he was dry to the touch, she asked him. "Would you like to play with Whiskey and Spike?" He cocked his head sideways, eying her, like he was contemplating her questions. He nudged her hand with his head in response, which Sarah took to mean *put me down.*

Whiskey and Spike were lying bellies down splayed on the floor, each with an end of the alligator plushie in their mouths.

As soon as Pierre's feet hit the floor, he took off toward Whiskey as fast as his short legs and build would let him. In a flying leap, he landed atop Whiskey's back and slurped the cattle dog's ear with his tongue.

Whiskey released the gator to look over his shoulder at his freeloading friend before shaking his body so that Pierre slid off him and onto the floor. Whiskey stood and mouthed Pierre's arm—his indication he wanted to play—and then took off running under the counter and into the backroom. Pierre tried to keep up. Spike ignored them and squeaked the gator, like he was happy to have the toy all to himself.

The door to the Coiffure opened and Tony, who lived with Spike and owned Big T's Fitness, walked in. His black puffy coat was unzipped and his black t-shirt clung to his broad chest. He wore black track pants and blue running shoes. "Hey, Sarah, Em, boys," Tony greeted.

"Hi, Tony. How's everything going?" Sarah placed Spike's leash on the counter.

"Busy. I'm releasing a new protein shake line next month and opening a new gym in Cedar Rapids on Valentine's Day. Spike and I have never been busier, between shooting the promos, making sure all the equipment will arrive in time, hiring the staff for the new place..."

"Wow. Sounds like a lot of work," Emily said.

"It is. But I wouldn't have it any other way. I love what I do." Tony pulled out his wallet and handed cash to Emily.

"That's how I feel about working here," Emily said. She was in her third year of school after finishing her associates degree last year. She had debated studying biology and then going to veterinary school but had decided that was too many years of education. Instead, she was studying animal nutrition and had talked with Sarah about the possibility of expanding the Coiffure's offerings to include bathing and grooming, teeth brushing, anal gland expressing, nail trimming, ear cleaning, detangling, and nutritional consultation so every animal they served could have diets that were best for their skin and coats.

"What flavors do you have in your new protein shake line?" Sarah asked.

"The usual chocolate, vanilla, and strawberry," Tony said, "but we've also made matcha, peanut butter, a mixed greens version so you can get your protein and smoothie in one, and a caffeinated protein and coffee mix. We have containers of pre-made shakes and jars of powders so you can mix it with your choice of milk or nondairy."

"Sounds like you've thought of everything," Sarah said. "I can't wait to try one."

"Spike's favorite is the peanut butter."

"Um," Emily frowned. "Tony, I'm pretty sure dogs aren't supposed to have protein shakes. Things in protein powder for humans, like whey or xylitol, can be harmful or even toxic to dogs."

"Really?" Tony connected Spike to his leash.

"Yes. Many dogs are lactose intolerant. Animal nutrition is what I'm studying in college."

"I had no idea," Tony said. "He laps the stuff up and has never gotten sick."

"Well, maybe he, specifically, isn't lactose intolerant, but I'd be cautious. Better to check with Dr. Schank." Dr. Schank was the only vet in Cottageville so most of the residents went to him instead of driving thirty minutes to the next town.

"Good thinking," Tony said, before pursing his lips and furrowing his brow like he was considering something. "I wonder if there is a market for dog-friendly protein shakes."

Sarah chuckled. "That's one thing I like about you, Tony. Your business mind is always churning." It wasn't common knowledge around town but Tony—who a number of people thought was all brawn and few brains—had an MBA from one of the top business schools in the country. Big T's brand of personal training, executive coaching, gyms and fitness studios, and related merchandise was an ever-growing empire that Tony used to do good in the world, including paying for renovations to the library after a big rig lost control and smashed through its plate glass windows in December and upgrading the jungle gym and playground equipment in Cottageville Park. Big T's sponsored the dog park, a Little League team, a girls' softball team, the uniforms for the high school football and basketball teams, and other things Sarah was sure few people knew anything about because while Tony was all about advertising his offerings, he kept most of his philanthropy on the downlow. And that, she respected. "So I guess since you're opening a new Big T's on Valentine's Day, you and Spike will miss the parade."

"Yes. I tried to figure out how to be there for the early morning open and then come back for the parade and then go back for the rest of the gym's first day, but it seemed like too much driving back and forth."

"I'm sure it would be," Sarah said. "We'll miss you. But what you are doing is exciting."

Tony smiled. "It is. I love seeing so many people transform themselves and their lives. The confidence they get when they feel better about themselves is inspiring. It never gets old for me."

"That's great," Emily said.

"Come on, Spike. "We've got a lot to do. Thank you both so much. And you, too, Whiskey." Tony scratched Whiskey's head, and then he and Spike went out the door.

"Who's next on today's schedule?" Sarah asked, while taking a sip of her now-cold coffee.

CHAPTER THREE

Hours later, Sarah and Whiskey were embraced by the comforting scent of marinara and bubbling cheese when they walked through their front door. "Hi, honey. I'm home," Sarah joked loud enough for Jared to hear. She assumed he was in command of her kitchen. Last year, when he had been hurt in an accident, he recovered at Sarah's house so he wouldn't be alone. After he had healed and they had decided to be a couple, she told him to keep her key. On days like today, she was grateful he had it and loved to cook, as that wasn't one of her favorite things.

He took a few steps toward the front door while saying, "Welcome home. How was your day?" Jared's grey cords and blue and black flannel shirt were covered by an apron with small Whiskey faces all over it. He was wiping his hands on a dish towel as he approached Sarah, bent, and pecked her lips with his. And then he knelt to give Whiskey a hug.

"Fine," Sarah said, hanging her coat on a rack by the door. "The usual. Though early this morning Bill volunteered himself and his grange brothers to help with the parade."

"That's great and should relieve you of some stress." Jared stood and started to follow Whiskey to the kitchen. Over his shoulder he called, "Do you want a glass of wine before dinner?"

Sarah trailed after him. "No. I haven't drunk enough water today so I'll stick with that. Do I have time to change?" Sarah felt like she carried the fur and dander of every animal she saw today on her sweater and jeans.

"Yes. Go make yourself clean and comfortable." He grinned. "I'll feed Whiskey and pull the lasagna out. It can sit for a few minutes while the garlic bread browns. Salad is already on the table, along with glasses of water. I'll meet you there when you are ready."

"You're the best." Sarah gave him a quick kiss before heading to her room.

Whiskey parked himself on his haunches next to his food bowl, patiently awaiting his evening meal.

As Sarah stripped off her clothes and stepped into the shower, she heard the sharp siren of a fire truck coming closer. The sound grew louder, and Sarah paused under the spray of warm water, her heart quickening. She rinsed off quickly, wrapped herself in a towel, and peered out the bathroom window. Through the fading light of evening, she could see the red and white flashes reflecting off the houses at the top of her street. White smoke curled faintly against the dark sky.

Pulling on a pair of sweatpants and an oversized hoodie, Sarah hurried back to the kitchen. "What's going on?"

The lasagna and the toasted garlic bread sat atop the stove, ready to be eaten. Jared had removed the apron from his clothes. "I'm not sure. I can't tell if it is one of the houses at the top of your street or something in the park. But whatever it is, it looks big."

Sarah nodded, her stomach twisting. "Maybe we should go out there," she started, but Jared held up a hand.

"Let me check it out. You stay here. Dinner's ready, your hair is wet, and there's not much we can do if the fire department is already on it." He squeezed her shoulder and exited the kitchen.

"Umm," Sarah started. She couldn't believe he expected her to stay there and wait. Did he not know her?

She followed after him as he grabbed his jacket from the rack. Sarah shoved her feet into her fleece-lined boots. She told Whiskey, who had raced them to the door, to stay, before she stepped out into the cold evening air.

"I said I'd go." Jared turned to her and frowned.

"I heard you," Sarah said. "But you know I'm not content to sit things out."

Jared chuckled. "Of course not." He reached for her hand and entwined his fingers with hers, and they set off up the sidewalk at a fast pace.

The orange glow from the fire could be seen from the top of Sarah's street. Crackles and pops could be heard over the indistinct voices of the fire fighters. Smoke rose like a disembodied spirit into the night sky. Sarah pinpointed the location of the blaze and realized that what they were hearing was the consumption and death of the big white pine that Mayor Trish lit every year at Winter Wonderland to launch the holiday season. As they got closer, they saw that branch by branch the tree was being destroyed, like forgotten memories.

Sarah let loose an involuntary moan as she stopped in her tracks and tears trickled down her face. Jared pulled her against his chest, and she felt his lips against her damp hair.

She had loved that tree, playing among its needles and trying to climb into its prickly arms as a young girl when she visited Gigi. It was braided into her memories of her grandmother. The pine was part of Cottageville's history, part of its community. *What on earth had caused it to burn?* Sarah was sure its sap and resin made it more flammable than other kinds of trees. *But trees didn't spontaneously combust. So what had happened?*

When Sarah pulled back from Jared's embrace to look at the tree one more time, she noticed some of her neighbors standing a safe distance away, beyond a perimeter the police had erected. Many of her friends looked awestruck and wore masks of grief and disbelief that Sarah was sure mirrored her own.

Leaning towards Sarah, Jared inquired, "Are you okay?" His eyes searched her face.

"I'm sad and frustrated. There's nothing we can do."

"That's true. But maybe it won't be a complete loss. Have you ever seen those trees that have been burnt by fire but still live? It's like they come back or resprout or something."

Sarah's eyes turned glossy with tears as she stared at the many-storied fire that was once the beloved pine. "I don't think that will be the case with this one." The emotional pain she felt made it difficult to breathe, or maybe that was the smoke. She grabbed Jared's arm and turned them around and took a few steps toward home. "Let's go hug Whiskey and eat the beautiful meal you made us. I've seen enough for today."

"As you wish, mi'lady."

Whiskey greeted them with a bark at the door before he sniffed their pant legs like a detective piecing together the mystery of where they had been through invisible clues. Sarah crouched to his level and hugged him around his red furred neck. "I love you, boy." She wiped the last of her tears with her hand before standing and taking off her boots and jacket.

Jared carried the lasagna and bread into the dining room. "Want me to reheat anything?"

Sarah shook her head and sat in a chair across from him. "At any temperature, it is still delicious." She snagged a hunk of garlicky goodness from the baking sheet and plopped it next to the rectangle of noodles and cheese Jared had placed on her plate. She served them both some salad on small coordinating plates.

"So, how was your day?" Sarah asked after swallowing her first couple of bites.

"Good. The PR people at the publisher emailed me today with a list of dates and interviews they've lined up in April around the release date of my book."

"That's exciting," Sarah said.

Jared had his first graphic novel coming out in two months, and he was busy working on his second and some commissioned art pieces in his free hours from working at Java and Juice. Sarah was so proud of him for following his dreams and for getting traction in his art career. He was super talented, and she was pleased Cottageville and the national publishing scene were recognizing his gifts.

"Is it all remote or will you be flying places? And at least if you are doing the PR in April it won't interfere with your annual trip to Comic Con."

"True. Some of it is remote, but they are talking about getting me on a couple of New York morning shows."

Sarah stopped with a forkful of lasagna halfway to her mouth. "Oh my gosh, Jared. That would be huge!"

"It would indeed, if they can pull it off."

"They will. I just know it. But then you'll get all famous and won't want to be with a lowly dog groomer like me," Sarah teased.

"You're not just a dog groomer. You're a kick-ass crime fighter and Whiskey's sidekick." Jared grinned.

"Uh, you've got some spinach in your teeth right here." Sarah ran a fingernail between her own top front teeth.

Jared repeated her actions. "Thanks for always having my back… or at least my smile."

"It's the least I can do."

Their banter was interrupted by the ringing of the doorbell. Whiskey ran to answer it and slid on the hardwood floors and slammed into the door. "Are you okay, dog?" Sarah patted his head as he stood. "You need to back up a bit so I can open the door."

Officer John Beams' black curls framed his uniform cap and his hazel eyes seemed to sparkle in the porch lights of Sarah's house. "Evening, Sarah. Jared." Beams nodded his head at them.

Whiskey pushed past Sarah to greet his friend.

"Give me five, Whiskey," Officer Beams commanded, holding out his right hand. Whiskey tapped John's fingers with his paw.

"Way to go." Officer Beams focused his attention back on Sarah. "I wondered what time you went through the park, Sarah. I know you and Whiskey walk it on your way home."

"We got home maybe ten or fifteen minutes before the fire truck sirens started. Why?"

Jared stood close behind Sarah and put his hand on her right bicep, but he said nothing.

"Did you see anyone in the park when you came through?"

"A mom I don't know was pushing a baby in a stroller on the path. They were bundled up against the cold. Do you want to come in?" Sarah could see John's breath as he spoke.

"No. This won't take long. You saw no one else?"

Sarah looked over John's shoulder into the darkness and searched her mind. When they entered from Main Street, no one was around. The air felt still, unlike the morning's whipping wind. But it was cold. Too cold for most people to enjoy the outdoors. Sarah was certain she saw nor talked to anyone. She and Whiskey speed-walked home, excited about the prospect of Jared's home-cooked meal. "I saw no one," she reiterated.

"Okay. Thank you," Officer Beams said.

"What's this about, John?"

He looked Sarah in the eyes and said, "We are in the very initial stages so please don't tell anyone. The fire investigator still needs to do the job, but the fire chief said they smelled an accelerant when they arrived at the scene."

"Arson?" Incredulousness oozed from Jared's voice.

"Who'd want to harm that tree?" Sarah asked.

"We don't know," Officer Beams admitted. "But we certainly plan to find out. Please think some more about your walk home. Maybe your subconscious registered something. A slight movement, something out of place, footprints, anything. If you think of something, give me a call. Enjoy the rest of your evening." He tipped his hat, turned, and walked back to his patrol car.

Sarah called Whiskey, who was using an azalea in the front yard as a urinal, back inside. Once the door was shut, she shook her head at Jared. "Why? Why would someone intentionally immolate a tree? I don't get it."

"People can be cruel. And they can be stupid, and some of them burn things because they like to watch fires or they have impulse control issues regarding the setting of fires."

"Or maybe they wanted to hear the voice of God," Sarah joked. "But seriously, a pine is a living, breathing thing. It deserved respect and care." Sarah knew she sounded a bit whiny and she hated that, but she was angry and confused and disgusted with humankind.

Jared wrapped his arms around her. "Maybe we should go finish dinner and then find something lighthearted to watch."

"I'm no longer hungry," Sarah mumbled. "But I'll sit with you while you finish eating and I'll do the clean-up after, since you cooked.

I'm really grateful for that, by the way. You take good care of me." She kissed his cheek and then released him, before walking back to the dining table.

"Want me to stay with you tonight?" Jared asked fifteen minutes later as he sopped up the last bite of sauce with a bit of garlic bread.

"Whiskey and I would like that," Sarah said. "I can't get that giant torch image out of my mind. I'm afraid I'll have nightmares."

CHAPTER FOUR

After a restless night's sleep, Sarah and Whiskey took their morning walk through the park, as usual. But this time, Sarah made an intentional stop at the charred remains of the white pine. She glanced once at what had been a vibrant, oxygen-exhaling tree that was now a black charcoal outline of its former self. It smelled of evergreen, campfire, and bog. The ground around the tree was squishy under a light crunch of ice. Sarah felt gutted to see something turn desolate, so she kept her focus on the ground, as they circled the evergreen. She knew the perimeter had been searched by the fire fighters and the police, but she wondered if they had missed anything, a scrap of paper or cloth, a footprint, a miniature can of lighter fluid.

Whiskey sniffed once at the tree carcass, before widening his perimeter to something less acrid, like the scent of squirrel or raccoon. He weaved around frozen blades of grass, crispy brown leaves and needles, and the cement path that wound its way to all of the wonder the park had to offer: the swing sets and jungle gym, ball fields, open fields where dogs romped and played catch, and the pavilioned picnic grove.

Ten feet from the tree, just outside the police perimeter tape, a glint of silver caught Sarah's eye in the early morning sun. Using her gloved hand, she bent and picked up a wrapper with Trident imprinted on a diagonal over and over. She brought the foil and paper rectangle to her nose. It smelt of cinnamon. She wondered who had dropped it? The arsonist? A firefighter? The police? Or was it one of last night's lookie-loos? Was it a clue?

Sarah placed the paper in her pocket but then second-guessed if she should leave it where she found it. *That was the problem when you didn't know if it was trash or part of the mystery of who torched the tree.*

Whiskey let loose a single bark and stood on his back legs with his front feet against an oak. He looked upward at a squirrel who taunted him with clicking sounds as it ran partway down the rough bark to him and then back up again, always staying outside the range of his reach.

"You having fun, boy?" Sarah asked, her breath vaporizing into white mist. *It sure was cold this morning.*

Whiskey ran to her and clamped onto her hand with his mouth. He guided her toward the oak with the squirrel, like he expected her assistance.

"I suck at squirrel hunting, Whisk. You know that."

He flashed his black mouth at her with a smile.

Scurrying was overheard so they looked up again as the squirrel raced down the tree at them. But it somehow lost its grip and fell right in front of Whiskey's face. He acted on instinct and picked up the squirrel with his mouth.

"No, Whiskey. Drop it," Sarah commanded.

Mr. Obedience opened his mouth and the squirrel tumbled onto the ground. It was still. Sarah didn't know if it was stunned, injured, or gone. She grabbed Whiskey by the collar and pulled him back a foot. They watched the squirrel in silence. It didn't move. It didn't even seem to inflate its sides to take a breath.

Tears filled Sarah's eyes. The death of the tree, the death of the squirrel, it seemed like too much on top of a stressful few months.

"Come on, boy," Sarah said. "Let's go see Jared and then get to work. We have another busy day." Whiskey raced up the path—squirrel forgotten—toward Main Street.

Java and Juice was packed this morning with townspeople at every table. Usually Whiskey ran straight to the counter regardless of who was in line, but this morning, he stayed at Sarah's side when he wasn't greeting their friends at the tables. Chief James' wife, a brassy blonde who made yoga clothes her daily uniform, was seated with her BFF Mayor Trish McGowan, and Sarah could hear them talking about the tree.

"It was the damnedest thing how quickly it burnt. Went up like an old stack of newspapers. Thank God the fire department responded as quickly as they did. But I don't think the tree has a chance of making it. Did you see it this morning?"

"No," Barbara said, taking a sip of her coffee from its porcelain Java and Juice logo'ed mug. "James was out until the wee hours with the fire chief."

"I'm sure. I was there for part of the time. I think I'm going to have to find money in the budget now to plant a new tree." Trish tsked.

"It can't be a young one," Barbara said.

"I know. We're gonna need a big one, fully grown, to light in ten months."

"Is it even tree-planting season?" Barbara asked, tearing a flaky, golden point from her croissant.

"I don't think so."

At that point, Sarah had a brainstorm. She got out of line and walked over to the table. "Excuse my eavesdropping," she addressed Barbara and Mayor Trish. "But would you like a donation booth or a game or something at the Valentine's Day Pet Parade to raise money to buy and plant a new tree? I'm sure we can think of something that will raise the needed money so it doesn't have to be taken from another part of the budget."

"What a fine idea, Sarah," Mayor Trish said. "Maybe we can stick with the theme and people can pay a dollar or fifty cents to hug a tree. A take on a traditional kissing booth which no one wants to do in a post-pandemic and MeToo movement world."

Barbara chuckled. "I'm not sure that's politically correct, but I do think the idea has tremendous potential. Get it? Tree-mendous?" She laughed at her own pun.

"That's a good one," Trish said. "My office can sponsor the booth. It's not too late, is it?"

"No," Sarah said. "I mean the vendor deadline is this week, but well, you're the mayor, so..." Her voice trailed off.

"So I can sign myself a permit and pay the fee and call it good."

"Exactly," Sarah said. "I'll assign you the spot near the old tree in the park. There's an oak already there that we can wrap a bow around and ask people to hug and take their photo. And if seeing the charred remains doesn't inspire people to pony up money, I don't know what will." Sarah pulled her phone from the back pocket of her jeans and made a note.

"Sounds good," Trish said. "Thank you, Sarah. You're always so solutions-oriented. It's awesome."

Sarah grinned and excused herself to get back in line to order black coffee for her to-go cup, two of those decadent cinnamon heart and dark chocolate chunk scones, and two of whatever the salad special was for the day. But this time, Whiskey cut the line, like he was tired of waiting. "Whiskey, get back here," Sarah said, embarrassed that her dog walked in front of three people and sat at attention at the counter.

"Whiskey, my man," Jared said, as he typed the customer's order into the computer. Sarah didn't know the man at the counter, but he was wearing a county fire jacket so she wondered if he was the fire inspector. For a split second she contemplated asking him and offering him the gum wrapper in her puffy coat pocket.

But he grabbed his coffee from Jared and bee-lined for the door, though not before Sarah saw the dark circles under his eyes and the weariness of a man who hadn't slept last night. She decided to talk to the Chief or Officer Beams first, instead of a man she didn't know.

When she got to the front of the line, Jared bowed and said, "Mi'lady. The usual?" And he reached for her travel mug.

"Yes, kind sir." She batted her eyes at him, tapped her card against the reader, and added a healthy tip.

Jared handed her the tumbler and a bag with her food, and he snuck Whiskey a second homemade chicken dog biscuit. He reminded Sarah he wouldn't see her tonight as he was hanging out with his friends, but that he would check in with her later.

Sarah said hellos and goodbyes to some of the patrons she knew who were having breakfast at Java and Juice before heading out the door and walking the four blocks to her business. The lights were on, but the door was still locked. Sarah could see Emily, in her black combat boots, tights, and a black velvet dress under the denim dog print apron, scrubbing the counter that separated the back room from the entry way or waiting area through the window.

When Sarah had her green door open, Whiskey wiggled his way next to Em and leaned into her leg.

"Oh Whiskey. Do you need a cuddle?" Emily asked.

The dog pushed harder against her.

She knelt to his level—which was knee high to her—and put one arm around his neck like she was putting him in a headlock. He strained toward her and slurped the side of her cheek with his big pink tongue.

"You're so funny. Have you had a good morning so far? You have chicken breath so you must have stopped at Java and Juice."

Before Whiskey could respond, Sarah rattled the paper bag with their scones and salads.

"What was the special salad today?" Emily stood to her full height, picked up the cleaning rag, and opened the hinged part of the counter so Sarah could walk through.

"Lemon pepper salmon with pickled onions and mixed greens."

"Sounds scrumptious. And if I haven't said so before, I'm grateful you get us lunch every day."

"It's one of the bennies of working with me," Sarah said. "I may not be able to pay the big bucks, but like those Silicon Valley tech companies, I can provide meals and snacks while you are on our magnificent campus." Sarah arced her arm and hand from left to right like Vanna White showing off all of the items on display.

"Was Java and Juice crowded? When I drove past on my way here, it looked like standing room only."

"Yes, the tables were all full. And it seemed like most people were talking about the fire."

"Have you seen it? The tree, I mean?"

Sarah put their salads in the refrigerator in the back room, put the scones and her coffee on the table, grabbed her apron off a hook, and put it on. "Jared and I went to see what all of the sirens were about last night. The blaze was huge, like twenty or thirty or forty feet in the air. It was crazy."

"Oh wow. Someone posted a video of it on the neighborhood message board. I could hear some pops and crackles and the roar of the flames. It was scary."

"It was. Even worse in person, I'm sure."

"Was anyone hurt?"

The question made Sarah pause. She hadn't considered it and had no idea. "I don't know." John Beams hadn't mentioned anyone getting hurt or being exposed to too much smoke inhalation.

"What do you think happened? People on the message board had all kinds of speculation, from someone getting too close to it with a cigarette to spontaneous combustion—which isn't a thing, by the way; I checked—to arson."

"It could have been an accident." Sarah frowned as she said the words and she twisted her bottom lip between two fingers.

"But you don't believe that," Emily said, picking up one of the scones and taking a big bite.

"I do not. Arson seems most likely with the way that it burnt. The tree was alive without any dead branches or dried out bits. The fire was too thorough, the destruction too extreme."

Emily's eyes narrowed as she said, "You think someone did something to the tree before lighting a match or building a fire under the bottom branches or however the hell it got on fire?"

The "yes" punctured Sarah's throat like a fish hook; she couldn't get it out. So she nodded her head once in answer.

"Any idea who or why?"

"Not a clue. But seeing the crispy black remnants this morning on my way here caused tightness in my chest and a lump in my throat like I had swallowed a big chunk of coal and it wouldn't go down."

"It feels personal." Emily's voice was barely above a whisper and held a reverence that surprised Sarah.

"It does. I have so many memories of visiting Gigi and climbing in that tree. It was as much my playmate as any of the kids I knew from my summers here. And now it is gone like her." Tears filled Sarah's eyes.

"Aww, Sarah. That's beautiful. And I totally get it. Here." Emily wrapped her arms around her boss.

And just as she did, Whiskey ran toward them to be included in the embrace, but he got sidetracked when the Coiffure's door opened, and in walked Taylor. From the top of his ski jacket poked the knobby green head of Iggy the iguana.

CHAPTER FIVE

"**S**orry to interrupt," Taylor said, shutting the door on the cold.

"Not at all," Sarah said in reflex.

"Hey, Em. Do you have time to trim Iggy's nails?" Taylor's black hair was standing on end today, twisted together in spikes. His skin was pale like Johnny Depp's in *Edward Scissorhands*. Like Emily, he favored clothes devoid of color, and occasionally painted his fingernails black. For the past year, Taylor and Emily had hung out a lot, and she had also hung out or dated Travis, the assistant to Sergio, the top hairdresser in Cottageville. Around the winter holidays, Emily realized she felt more sibling than significant other to Taylor.

"Sure, T. You off today?" Since Jared's accident in early December, Taylor had been filling in at Java and Juice. His hours had been cut once Jared was well enough for full-time, but Taylor still clocked in twenty hours a week plus studied at the nearby junior college. Taylor slid all two and a half feet of Iggy from inside the heater of his jacket and placed him on the counter. Iguanas hated cold weather, so Taylor did everything he could to keep his best buddy warm and happy.

Emily pulled nail clippers from her apron pocket and snipped the tips from Iggy's claws.

"He scratched me yesterday," Taylor said, pushing up his sleeve to show her the fine red line on his wrist.

"I hope you put peroxide or rubbing alcohol on it."

"Nah. It's all good." Taylor grinned at her.

"Reptiles and dog and cat scratches can cause infection," Emily insisted as she finished Iggy's left back foot.

"It looks okay to me." Taylor shrugged. He pulled a ten and a couple of ones from his pocket and handed the money to Emily. "Wanna game tonight?"

"I can't tonight, but I could on Friday."

"Sounds good. I'll order pizza."

"K."

Taylor placed Iggy's feet against his chest and then zipped his jacket all the way up. He held the iguana with one hand and opened the Coiffure door with the other.

When the door was shut again, Sarah said, "You know he still has a thing for you, right?"

"We're friends."

"I know that. And you know that. But Taylor, he's still hoping for something more."

"I'm not leading him on. I've been clear. What he thinks or hopes is on him. And I don't mean that in a mean way."

"I know you don't."

"So back to the tree for a moment." Emily took a swig of coffee. "I think you think it is arson. Does that mean we are going to investigate?" She raised one eyebrow at Sarah, which made Sarah laugh.

"You look like an anime character."

"Which one?"

"I don't know. I don't know any of their names, except that Totoro. But any of those dark haired girls with big eyes."

"Yeah, that's most of them...unless they are blonde or red-heads. Or have blue or purple hair. But they all have big eyes."

"That's as much clarity as a swamp. Anyway, I would love to investigate. But other than around the tree I don't know where to start. Did you see anything on the message boards? Did someone act like they knew more than others?"

"No. But I wasn't looking at that or social media for that. I will go back and see and let you know." Emily finished her scone. "Those are so good."

"I know it. I told her to sell them at the parade along with those sugar cookies she makes around this time of year. You know, the ones iced and piped to look like candy hearts?"

"Last week, I helped Taylor come up with more modern sayings for those cookies. We laughed until we almost wet ourselves coming up with slogans. 'You've bumbled your way to my heart.' 'Be right. Swipe right.' Those aren't some of the better ones, but the others are a surprise."

"I can't wait to see them. By the way, you seemed to be scrubbing that counter pretty hard when I walked in the front door. What happened?"

"Oh, George stopped by with Chutney. He had taken him out for a walk and the dog rolled in something so he brought him here for a bath, but apparently Chutney and I felt the same about seeing each other. He did his Tasmanian devil act and shredded George's hands. Blood splattered on the counter before I could don the gloves and take the little demon. Instead, George said something about seeking medical treatment and took the dirty dog with him out the door. I removed the blood with some cold water and watered-down bleach. Drops went the whole way to the door."

"Wow. Sorry I wasn't here to help."

"No worries. I came in early for a quiet place to study. I need to take an exam after work today and I don't feel quite ready."

Sarah looked at their schedule for the day: a steady stream of big dogs with many layered coats. Sebastian the St. Bernard was due any minute with his human Scott Simon. If they tag-teamed him on the bath, Sarah could handle the trimming, drying, and grooming so Emily could look over her notes. Sebastian was a calm and gentle soul. The more lively Annabelle the akita was due in before lunch, followed by Max, a thick-coated silver and white malamute, and Homer, a rescued husky who, with his human retired national park ranger Dennis Denali, were some of Cottageville's newest residents, as they had moved into the area four months before.

Sarah made a note in the schedule to call Daniel during her lunch. She still had no idea what he needed help with or what kind of timeline he had planned for the proposal.

She turned to tell Emily that they could make time for her to study, when the door to the Coiffure opened and Whiskey wildly raced like a kitten who had mainlined catnip to greet the next guests.

"A for enthusiasm right there," Emily said.

"He's such a funny dog. Hey, Sebastian. Who's your friend?"

Instead of being trailed by Scott Simon, the big boned, brown and white dog had a model-thin, well-dressed blonde woman attached to the loop end of his leash.

"Samantha Simon, Scott's sister," the woman answered. She reached out her hand for a shake.

"Hi, I'm Sarah and this is Emily. And that's Whiskey, who takes his job as greeter more seriously than those guys at Walmart."

Samantha threw her head back and released a throaty guffaw, which caught Sarah off guard. "Scott tore his meniscus and had to have surgery, and since he has been single since Christmas, I flew into town to take care of him and this big guy."

"Ooo. How's he doing?" Sarah asked.

"That sounds painful," Emily said.

"He's recovering. He doesn't deal well with pain, but he's a dude and a lot of them don't." She flashed what Sarah was sure were recently bleached teeth.

"But he gets to start PT on Monday. So that's a good thing. And once he's well enough to walk this big lug, my work here will be done and I can go home to Lalaland." She handed the leash to Sarah. "Scott said two hours. Is that right?"

Sarah looked over Sebastian to make sure he wasn't matted or had anything going on besides the usual. He didn't look like he had been brushed this week, but that was okay. "Two hours should be fine. Or two and a half or three if you want more time for yourself." Whiskey always relished as much time as he could get with his friends.

"That's sweet. Okay. I'll be back around lunchtime. Tootles." And she waved on her way out the door.

"She's spunky," Sarah said.

"That's funny. Not a word you or I would usually use. But it certainly fits. Come on, Sebastian, walk this way and into the tub." Emily grabbed the leash from Sarah and led the dog under the counter and into the back. Whiskey walked behind him, a little to the left, like he was walking point and covering Sebastian's back.

As soon as the warm water hit Sebastian's fur, he did what he always did: he shook and sprayed water in a six-foot radius. Whiskey ran to the front room and out of the blast zone. Sarah and Emily turned their backs for a second so their faces didn't bear the brunt of the flying H2O. When they turned around, Sarah clamped her hands at two points on Sebastian's spine, in an effort to keep him from shaking again. Emily maneuvered the hose to get him as wet as possible before they added the shampoo. Bathing Sebastian was best as a two-person or more job, which is why Scott Simon didn't attempt it at home.

Ten minutes and two more shakes later, the rinse water ran clear over the dog, signaling all of his suds had gone down the drain. They draped three shower sheets over Sebastian's massive body and led him to the grooming area, where Whiskey joined them once again. Sarah towel dried Sebastian before brushing his fur and starting the blow dryer.

Emily, sitting at the break table allegedly studying, yelled over the noise of the blow dryer, "Hey, Sarah. Chief James posted on the neighborhood message board asking if any homes near the park have security footage that shows people coming in or out of the park."

"Did he specify a timeframe?"

"Any time between five and six."

"Hmph." Sarah had gotten home from work yesterday at five-thirty, and she was almost certain the parts of the park she walked through were empty. "Did anyone respond saying they have a Ring camera or anything?"

"Not to the public forum. But he included a phone number for people to call. Do you have a doorbell camera or any security cameras on your property?"

"Both Jared and John Beams wanted to install them when I received those threats last year. Jared put a camera on my porch, but I don't think it's been activated or wired-in or something."

"What's the point of having it if you aren't going to use it?"

"There isn't one. I'll ask him about it the next time I see it. I kind of forgot about it after that guy was caught."

"Good plan."

At that moment, the phone in Sarah's apron vibrated. She turned off the fur dryer and pulled out the phone. Daniel's name showed on the screen. "Hey, Daniel. What's up?"

"Is it a good time?"

"Well, I'm finishing up a St. Bernard. Can I call you back in ten minutes? Will that work for you?"

"Yes. I want to finish the conversation we started yesterday."

"Sounds good. I'll call you as soon as I'm done with Sebastian."

"Thanks."

Sarah smiled at her phone. She wondered what he was up to and how he planned to surprise her BFF, as Sarah was sure he would.

CHAPTER SIX

Just as Sarah let Sebastian free to play with Whiskey, the Coiffure's front door opened and Annabelle, who looked like caramel had been dripped on her beautiful thick fur, walked in alongside her human, Drake Farmer. Both Whiskey and Sebastian ran to greet them. Annabelle stood stock still while Sebastian sniffed her. And Sarah felt a bit of tension in the room. While Annabelle and Whiskey got along well, Sarah knew akitas could be territorial and needed to be dominant. But when the St. Bernard wagged his tail almost hitting Whiskey with it and Whiskey didn't react, Annabelle must have decided the brawny dog was okay as she, too, swished her tail.

"Sarah, do you have Valentine's Day bandanas?" Drake asked.

"I've decided we will participate in the parade. But let's face it, she's really not the costume type."

Sarah chuckled. "It would certainly ruin her security dog image to dress as Cupid. Here are the options." She pulled the stack of large and extra large size bandanas and flipped through them: royal purple background with colorful hearts; black background with red, pink, and white hearts; black background with big red and pink lip prints like the bandana had been kissed a lot; light blue background with candy hearts with words in a variety of pastel colors; and a red background with the word LOVE in cursive script to hang under the dog's chin.

Drake chose the purple with the hearts. "The purple feels royal like her ancient Japanese lineage. And the purple will compliment her sienna fur."

"Good choice then. If you could give us a couple of hours..." Sarah's voice trailed off.

"Of course. See you around two." As Drake opened the door to exit the Coiffure, Samantha Simon was standing on the other side. Sarah noticed Drake's posture stiffening at the stunning woman, who offered him a hearty, "Hey, there," which seemed to relax him a bit.

He responded, "Well, hello," and held the door so she could enter.

Sebastian barreled toward her as she said, "Whoa, big guy."

And Drake joked from behind her, "Are you talking to me?" which, given his resemblance to a willow tree, garnered a guffaw from Samantha, who turned around and said, "I like you. Samantha Simons. And you are?" She held out her hand.

"Drake Farmer. Pleased to meet you, ma'am."

They shook hands as Samantha said, "Ma'am. Do I look like an old lady to you?" Her smile could eclipse the sun.

"No, ma'am. I mean, No, Samantha."

Samantha guffawed again. "Are you single?" But before Drake could answer, she plowed forward with, "How'd you like to buy me a cup of coffee once I return this beautiful beast to its master?"

"Umm, I'd like to. Do you know Java and Juice? It's a few blocks from here. I could meet you there in half an hour."

"That sounds like a plan, Drake. I'll see you there. Thank you."

Drake gave a single nod, looked down at his watch, and then exited the Coiffure.

Sarah was amazed at how Samantha went after what she wanted, a bit like a shark that smelled blood.

Without asking how much the services were, Samantha put some cash on the counter. "Scott said he missed seeing you, Sarah. Sebastian looks fluffier and smells great." She sniffed the top of his head and ran her fingers through his fur.

"Tell him I hope he heals quickly. It's been a pleasure meeting you."

"Likewise. Come on, big boy. Let's go see your dad." She took hold of Sebastian's leash and led the dog out the door.

Emily had corralled Annabelle and Whiskey into the back, and Annabelle now stood in a walk-in tub ready for her bath. "Don't forget to call Daniel."

"Thanks for the reminder. With all of the in and out, it slipped my mind."

"I'll bathe Annabelle and you can eat your salad after you get off the phone."

"Thank you, Em."

Sarah grabbed her lunch from the refrigerator as she waited for Daniel to pick up the call. But instead of answering, her call went to voicemail. "Hey, Daniel. Sorry for the delay. I finally got free. Give me a call when it is convenient. Thank you."

She sat at the back room table and enjoyed a few moments of silence and calm as she ate, and she got halfway through the container of salad when her phone rang. "Daniel, thank you for calling me back."

"I couldn't answer before, Sarah, because Chief James and Chief Hannah were here." Hannah Beau led the Cottageville Fire Department as its first female chief. She and her husband Hunter Byrd, and their two adopted five-year-old daughters, Bao and Ai, were beloved members of the community.

"Oh, was it as part of the fire investigation?"

"Yes. They wanted sales records for anything that could be used as an accelerant. You know, like turpentine, road flares, petroleum jelly, acetone, lighter fluid, and the like."

"Wait, Vaseline is an accelerant?"

"It can be."

"Do you actually have records on those types of sales?"

Sarah mentally saw him shrug when he said, "Eh, depends. We have records attached to our inventory when something is scanned during check out. Whether or not we can track who bought it is another story. If a credit card was used, maybe. If cash was paid, we're out of luck, unless one of my workers remembers someone. Narrowing down all possible accelerants that we sell is the first challenge since so many household products could be used. Even rubbing alcohol or nail polish remover, paint thinner, or insecticides. I asked Hannah if the fire investigator can be more specific once the results from the lab are in. That would make my job easier."

"Wow. And of course, there's a possibility that whatever was used to start or encourage the fire wasn't bought at your store in the first place. It could have come from a gas station, someone's garage or shed, or from outside of Cottageville."

"That's true, too."

"Sounds like they have their work cut out for them."

"They always do. You know how investigations work. You've been part of few now." Daniel chuckled.

"True. Though one of the last ones wasn't by choice."

"Mysteries do seem to have a way of finding you, Sarah."

Sarah smiled at the phone even though Daniel couldn't see her. "Anyway, I believe you wanted to talk to me about Ginger."

"I did indeed. I would love to take her away on a picnic on Sunday, to where we went on our first date. But when we get back to our house—probably around four—I'd love to have all of our friends there to celebrate with us."

"You're sure she's saying, yes?" Sarah joked.

"I'm counting on it. And I'd like to count on you and Jared to invite the people and take care of the food and beverages. I'll reimburse you for everything. But I want this to be a surprise for Ginger so have everyone park back behind our bar or at the far end of our property or have them carpool so we don't pull up and she knows immediately what's going on. I'd love for it to really be a surprise when we walk through our front door. I know it's kind of last minute and you have a lot on your plate with the parade, but do you think you can do this? I'm fine if you want to order a stack of pizzas or whatever. Make it easy. Oh, and I picked up the bubbly already and hid it in our garage in the bottom box next to the old freezer."

Sarah made a note on a scratch piece of paper. "Do you have a guest list?"

"Nah. Invite the usual."

"But the whole town will want to be there. They have for much of both of your lives."

Daniel barked a familiar laugh. "That's true. And I'm grateful to everyone so feel free to spread the word."

"Okay. But maybe you should blindfold her before you pull up the house. That may be the only way to keep her from seeing everyone if the amount of people I think will want to be there show up."

"Point taken."

"And besides, there are many curious Cottageville minds that want to see what you've been doing at the farm for the past six months."

Daniel laughed loudly this time. "Good thing we're mostly done then. At least for now."

"So have everyone there by four. We will do that. I'm so happy for you both, Daniel. It will be such a joyous occasion."

"Thank you, Sarah. I appreciate your enthusiasm and your help."

"Oh, hey, since they will know they are coming to celebrate

your engagement, in case anyone asks, what should I tell them about gifts?"

"Oh. Gifts. I didn't think about that. You can tell them gifts are unnecessary. But if someone insists, maybe suggest seeds and related items or plants. We plan to plant a big veggie and herb garden once the ground stays thawed."

"Okay, sounds good. Thank you."

"No, thank you, Sarah. I'm sure you'll make our special day even more memorable. I have to go now. One of the cashiers just paged me."

"Okay, Daniel. Have a good afternoon." Sarah disconnected. She finished the rest of her salad and texted Jared, "We have a secret mission for Daniel. Can you stop by the Coiffure after work?"

Five minutes later came Jared's reply, "Affirmative. And color me intrigued."

Sarah grabbed a piece of paper from the printer and went into the grooming area. She told Emily, who was finishing rinsing Annabelle, about her call with Daniel and the semi-impromptu party. "Are you and maybe Taylor and Travis free on Sunday afternoon?"

"I am, and I'm sure Taylor wouldn't want to miss it. I'll check with him and with T."

"Please remind Taylor not to say a word to Ginger. I don't think he'd intentionally ruin the surprise, but I could see him saying something without thinking, like if he works on Saturday telling her he'll see her tomorrow even though she isn't working that day or something."

"Yeah, that's totally something he'd do. I'll reiterate."

"Thanks. And who else do you think we should invite?" Sarah had her pen poised over the paper.

"Didn't Gladys have them both in class?"

"Yes. Or at least I know Ginger took art. But Daniel may have too. Regardless, she knows his parents and has known him from birth."

"You'll have to invite both Daniel's and Ginger's parents, too."

"Oh that's probably true. But I wonder if he wants family there or only friends. I should have asked. You'd think if he wanted family, his mom could have planned this for them."

"Text him and ask."

"Okay." Sarah sent the text and while she awaited an answer, she added Bill, Chief James and Barbara, Mayor Trish, Daphne Smith, Emily, Taylor, Travis, Hannah and Hunter, John Beams and Braidington Bradley, and Candace Grimes to the list.

Daniel responded with a call, "Hey, Sarah. Great question. I was figuring it would be a friends celebration, but I guess since there's a huge age range of our friends because of our history and our businesses, maybe we should include the family. Then again, if it gets too big, someone is bound to say something to Ginger and then it won't be a surprise. Maybe we should keep it small and intimate. You and Jared, Emily and her two guys, John and Braidington if John is off that day, Candace if she's off. I'd love Gladys and Bill and Janice to come, but maybe if we invite the older generation then we have to include our parents and widen the circle. What do you think?"

"Let's let Sunday be just the closest friends and colleagues. How about I throw a town-wide engagement party for you in a few months, when the weather is better and you have added things to a gift registry."

Daniel smirked. "Okay. Sounds better and more manageable."

"It's all manageable," Sarah said. "I've got it under control. I'll text people right now and stress that it's a surprise. Thanks." She disconnected. "So, Em, we're keeping it small, a dozen people tops and swearing everyone to secrecy."

"Are you planning on decorating? You know, balloons, streamers, a she said 'yes' or 'congratulations' banner?"

"I haven't gotten that far in the planning. If I order pizzas maybe they can write stuff in the toppings, you know like arrange the pepperoni into a HELL YES."

"That'd be funny." She towel dried the akita, who wriggled against the terrycloth like a cat scratching its back against a post.

Sarah made a mental note to check social media for creative engagement party ideas when she was done with work. She wanted the party she threw both this weekend and at a later date to be as memorable as a first kiss.

CHAPTER SEVEN

The next couple of hours were busy with two drop-in nail clippings as well as the scheduled big dog baths. Sarah, Emily, and Whiskey—who never neglected his emotional support animal duties—worked nonstop until the door opened at three and Jared came in. Whiskey ran to greet him, and Jared scratched under his chin. Dark purplish half moons cast shadows under Jared's eyes and his shoulders were more slumped than usual.

Sarah kissed his cheek, as she was forearms deep in shampoo suds and dog, and asked, "Are you feeling okay, my lord?"

"The deliberate destruction of the tree has gotten to me, mi'lady, as well as the constant chatter about it. Everyone has a theory and a lot of people are pissed off.”

“Rightfully so. But I have some cheerful news. Daniel is popping the question and it’s all hush hush. He’s asked us to plan a small celebratory gathering at his house for four o’clock on Sunday. We are to yell ‘Surprise’ or ‘Congratulations’ or something when they walk through the door and then uncork the bubbly and party.”

“I like having something to celebrate.”

“Me too. It’ll be a small group. About ten or a dozen. Daniel already bought the champagne and told me where it is hidden. He said he’ll reimburse the food, etc.”

“Unnecessary.” Jared waved his hand dismissing the idea. “Should we go the barbecue route or pizzas, or were you thinking something more, like a sit-down dinner?”

“I’m thinking as easy and fun as possible so we can all enjoy ourselves.”

“Sounds like a plan. What tasks am I being assigned?”

“Beer for one, since I know nothing about it.” Sarah grinned.

“Beer I can handle. We could just get Daniel’s favorite and make everyone drink that. But I am guessing you want a variety of dark and light. Who all is coming to this shindig?”

Sarah ran through the friends list. “Do you think we should send an electronic invitation, phone that group of people, or send a text?”

“Electronic invite would look the best, unless you want me to create an image invite that you could then text or email. Do you have everyone’s email addresses?” Jared’s green eyes searched hers.

“No. I actually don’t. So that makes the decision for me. Do you mind creating a graphic and doing the invite layout? Do you have time this afternoon so we could send it today? We already don't have much time as Sunday is days away. People may already be busy."

"Yes, I can go home now and do it. I'll make the headline 'It's a Surprise' so everyone knows to keep their mouths shut."

Sarah laughed. "Sounds good. And thank you, my talented artist." She smacked her lips against his.

"My pleasure. Or it will be when you pay me in more of those kisses," Jared joked.

"What a bargain! I'm thinking pizzas, a giant salad, and maybe cupcakes that spell CONGRATULATIONS, DANIEL & GINGER. One letter per cupcake and that will be more than two dozen so guests can have more than one. I can make those on Sunday morning."

"Let me stay over on Saturday night and I'll help you." Jared's eyebrows were raised.

"Sounds good. I'm thinking of carrot cake and cream cheese frosting since that's Ginger's favorite."

"What's Daniel's favorite?"

Sarah pursed her lips and looked up in the air toward the right, thinking. "I don't think I know." She pulled out her phone and texted him. "What's your favorite cake flavor?"

"Black forest," was his immediate response. Sarah repeated the answer aloud.

"So half the batch will be that and half carrot cake?"

"I guess so."

"If you place an order with Produce and More for Saturday pick-up, I can swing by and get it on my way to your house." Jared knew Sarah had a vintage Jeep CJ but she walked almost everywhere;

whereas, he lived too far on the outskirts of town to walk to work every day. In the warmer months, he sometimes biked, but the weather had been too cold and windy since the end of autumn. "Anything else you need me to do between now and Saturday?"

"Maybe give me another kiss." Sarah grinned.

"Not again," Emily mumbled, which Sarah overheard.

"Sorry, Em." Jared said as he leaned over and kissed Sarah one more time before saying, "All right then. I'll see you tomorrow."

"Love you," Sarah called as Whiskey walked Jared to the door.

Sarah started to draft a grocery list for the party, but before she put more than three words into the notes section of her phone, the door to the Coiffure opened and her next client walked in. The rest of the afternoon the Coiffure was abuzz with activity of their regulars and people looking for a little extra pet pampering in preparation for the Valentine's Day parade even though it was ten days away.

At five thirty as Sarah was moving the load of towels from the washer to the dryer and Emily was taking out the trash, Sarah's phone rang. She glanced at the screen before answering, "Hey, G."

"Sarah, what are you doing for dinner tonight?"

"No plans. Why?"

"I made a giant pot of chili and cheese and jalapeno cornbread, but Daniel just texted he has to stay late at work. You and Whiskey want to come over and eat?"

"Oooo, that sounds delicious. We are leaving work soon and need to run home to get the car. See you at six?"

"Sounds good. See you then."

"Need me to bring anything?"

"Just your appetite."

Sarah chuckled. "Will do." She took one last look around to make sure they had done everything they needed to do. She thanked Emily for another fabulous day, turned off the lights, locked the door, and headed up the sidewalk.

But then she heard Emily call after her, "Hey, Sarah, do you want me to drive you home? It will save you a few minutes."

"Oh, thanks." Sarah held the backdoor open so Whiskey could jump onto the backseat of the Honda. "You ready for the test?" she asked Em.

"Yes. Thanks for the extra study time."

"No problem." In five minutes, Emily pulled into Sarah's driveway and they said goodnight.

Whiskey raced into the kitchen and hit his bowl with his paw making the metal clang against the hardwoods like a cymbal crashing in an empty concert hall. "I'm on it, dog. Have some patience." Sarah grabbed her cattle dog's raw food from the freezer and put a serving of it in a microwavable bowl to thaw it. When it was soft, she emptied the contents into Whiskey's bowl and it was eaten before she could inhale and exhale a breath.

"You really shouldn't eat so fast," Sarah said, knowing the words and the concepts behind them mattered little to her life companion. He'd eat however he wanted to. Fortunately for them both, cattle dogs had hearty digestive systems, unlike boxers, shih-tzus, some terrier breeds, and Great Danes, which had notoriously sensitive stomachs.

Sarah let Whiskey outside to do his business while she chose clean jeans, a t-shirt, and her alma mater's Husky sweatshirt to change into once she showered all of the dog hair and dander from herself. She left Whiskey back in before she stepped into the shower. At seven minutes to six, they locked the front door and climbed into the CJ for the ten-minute drive to Daniel and Ginger's rehabbed farmhouse.

As they drove up the driveway, the two-story home glowed warmly in the fading twilight, its wide front porch adorned with strings of soft white lights that twinkled like stars against the rustic wood beams. The white porch railings almost glowed against the house's blue-gray painted siding. Smoke curled from the big stone chimney, promising the cozy embrace of a roaring fire inside. Whiskey perked up in the back seat, his ears swiveling toward the faint bark of another dog somewhere in the distance.

Sarah hopped down from her Jeep as Whiskey barreled over her seat to make his own escape from the vehicle. "Geez, dog. Impatient much?" She shook her head as Whiskey beelined up the stairs and onto the wooden front porch. Standing on the front porch felt to Sarah like stepping onto the cover of a lifestyle magazine—a picturesque retreat from everyday life, and unlike in much of Cottageville, the neighbors' houses were barely in sight through the trees.

Sarah eyed the new brass doorbell, running the tip of her pointer finger over the cold metal. The bee shape was whimsical as well as classic and so beautiful. Sarah wanted one for her own home. She pushed the button and heard the melodic sounds of a handbell ringing. It was so much better than the buzz sound hers made that she and Whiskey both hated.

The oversized front door opened and Ginger threw her arms around her BFF. "So glad you are here," she said.

Whiskey gave a sharp bark like "don't forget about me," and Ginger laughed before bending over to give him the attention he craved. She scratched between his ears and along his spine before handing him a homemade chicken biscuit she pulled from a pocket of the apron that covered her green wool sweater and jeans.

"Follow me," she said over her shoulder as she went from her foyer through the living room and into the kitchen.

Sarah took off her shoes near the front door, and then dropped her winter jacket and purse on a kitchen bar stool. When she looked back up, Ginger was passing her a glass of deep burgundy wine. "Zinfandel. Supposed to complement the spices. We'll see."

Sarah breathed in the nose of the wine before taking a sip. "Spicy on the finish."

Ginger nodded. "I figured we'd eat here, at the counter." Two places had already been set with dark red linen place mats and navy blue with white flowers oversized napkins. White plates holding a chunk of golden corn bread studded with cheddar and tiny green squares of pepper sat to the left side of the plate. Ginger filled two bowls with chili and set those on the plates next to bread before she came around to Sarah's side of the counter and sat down.

"Cheers," Sarah said, holding her stemless wine glass aloft. "To spending time together."

"Salut." Ginger touched her glass to Sarah's, and then they both took a sip, before dunking spoons into the chili.

Sarah swallowed her first bite. "Mmmm. So good."

"Thank you. So besides hosting the pet parade, what are you and Jared doing for Valentine's Day?"

"No clue. I'll probably be too tired to do anything after I get through the festivities. Did you know that almost two hundred pets are registered to strut down Main Street and through the park? Two hundred. I didn't even know Cottageville had so many household animal residents."

"I'm sure we have more than that. Don't most small children have goldfish and hamsters? I know I did as a kid. But of course, I wouldn't have taken those kinds of pets to a parade."

"No one has registered a goldfish or a hamster yet. But I do have one guinea pig, though I'm not sure if it will be walking on its own or riding atop its human's shoulder. Same with the iguana named Iggy and the arachnids and other non-canine pets."

"Got any pigs, potbelly or otherwise?" Ginger broke off some cornbread and dipped it into the chili before popping it into her mouth.

"One, I think. I've kind of lost track. We created an online registration system, and I have to admit that since the fire I haven't checked it. So I'm not even sure what the count is at the moment. My mind has been preoccupied."

"Understandable. Is there a cut off for people to participate in the parade?"

"Yes, registration ends this Friday at five p.m. You gonna adopt a pet before then and join us?"

"Very funny. More like I'm trying to figure out how much merchandise to have at our booth. Unlike Winter Wonderland where we've done this every year, this is new. I'd hate to bake too much or too little."

Sarah swallowed her latest spoonful of chili before saying, "I'd expect most of the town to come out, just like for Winter Wonderland. I think the novelty of it alone will draw a crowd, not to mention the pairings of people with their pets."

"Okay."

"What are you doing for Valentine's Day besides manning your booth?"

"Since it is a Saturday this year, both Daniel and I will be working. But that's okay. Every day is Valentine's Day for us."

"Awww," Sarah teased, "that's so sweet I feel one of my molars decaying."

"Ha ha. But I am serious. I never expected to have a love like this. He's a good guy."

"He definitely is."

"I have to show you what he gave me. Be right back." Ginger slid down from her high stool and padded up the wooden staircase.

Sarah polished off the chili in her bowl and lapped up any remaining juice by using the cornbread as a sponge. Everything was so delicious she wanted to ask Ginger for the recipe. As she took a sip of wine, Ginger appeared before her with a deep blue velvet box about eight inches square.

"Check this out," Ginger said, opening the hinged box top.

Nestled into velvet padding was a stunning diamond and sapphire necklace. None of the stones were huge. The chain was a row of small diamonds set in white gold, and the center focal point was the kind of flower outline a child might draw of petals with a round floret in the center. The petals were outlined in sapphires and the interior floret was a cluster of diamond chips.

"Holy cow. That's exquisite. Daniel got you that?" Sarah felt like her eyes were bugged out like a cartoon character's.

"He and his mother gifted it to me. It was his grandmother's and she died last year. Though it may have originally been her mother's." Ginger frowned in thought. "Anyway, it has been in his family, and as of last week, its care was entrusted to me."

Sarah ran her fingertip over a row of diamonds. "It really is breathtaking. Have you worn it yet?"

"Oh sure, every day," Ginger joked. "I'm actually afraid to wear it, if I'm honest. I mean, what if the clasp breaks or a diamond falls out or someone rips it from my neck." Ginger shuddered.

"I understand, though on that last part, the odds of someone ripping it from your neck here in Cottageville would be rare. The crime rate is pretty low."

"Said the woman who helped solve the last, what is it, four or five major crimes here?"

"You know what I mean. But maybe before you wear it, take it to a jeweler's to have the settings checked. Make sure nothing is loose."

"That's a great idea."

"Now can you put it on for me? I want to see how incredible you look."

Ginger grinned and put it around her neck and struck a pose.

"Gorgeous. Even more gorgeous than usual."

Ginger fluttered her eyelashes and held out her hand to be kissed. "Thank you. Thank you very much. You're too kind." And then she took off the necklace, returned it to the box, and ran it back upstairs.

Sarah helped Ginger load the dishwasher, and then Whiskey

and Sarah said goodbye since they knew Ginger had to be up at three a.m. to start baking the goodies at Java and Juice.

That night, as Sarah closed her eyes to sleep she kept envisioning Ginger's new heirloom, the sapphires and diamonds glowing against the dark blue velvet background like stars in the night sky.

CHAPTER EIGHT

The next few days were super busy as Sarah walked Whiskey every morning and afternoon, packed her schedule with canine clients, and sent out the final schedule and set up expectations to the vendors for the Valentine's Day festivities. The parade would start promptly at nine a.m. at the bottom of Main Street and trail up the central corridor, which would be closed to traffic for half the day, into Cottageville Park and end at the grandstand, an elevated platform that was usually next to the tree lit at Christmas. But for this event, Sarah had moved it to ten feet from the tree so the Mayor's hug a tree campaign could be nearest the burnt out pine. Sarah hoped its sight melted hearts and opened the wallets of the townsfolk.

Bill had assured Sarah that he and his brothers would be at the park by six a.m. to assist with booth set up, vendor check-in, and parade participant check-in. He also assured her that he had had calls with both the mayor's office and the local waste management company to double check on when the additional garbage receptacles would be added to the parade route and to the park. With all of those pets and their people meandering up Main Street, along with the high school marching band, and some floats from neighborhood organizations that wanted to promote their love, no one wanted to dampen spirits or waft unsavory smells by stepping in or carrying a hot deposit of poo.

Bill said he arranged for the plastic lined, tall cardboard box trash containers to be outfitted with a roll of pet waste bags, available to anyone who might need one.

"Thank you for thinking of this, Bill," Sarah had said that morning as Whiskey stopped on Bill's porch for his treat.

"If you think of anything else you need, please let us know," Bill said. "We want this event to be a success."

"Me, too," Sarah said.

It was now Saturday, late afternoon. Emily had left work ten minutes ago, and Sarah mopped the floor of the Coiffure after a nonstop day of too many muddy paws from the thawed ground. They had one more week of back-to-back bookings from people trying to get their pets looking their best for the parade. Sarah wondered if any of her client's companions planned to wear costumes or coordinated Valentine's day outfits. She could totally envision Daphne Smith dressing as a giant heart and Pierre donning a cupid costume, or Hannah Beau's beautiful adopted Chinese daughters Ai and Bao getting into the holiday spirit with their shih-tzu.

Looking forward to the festivities and seeing the joy on the faces of people of all ages was what was keeping Sarah going, because if truth be told, she was exhausted. And yet somehow, she had agreed to make dozens of cupcakes tomorrow morning and host the surprise party for Ginger. At least it wasn't at her house so she didn't have to worry about cleaning.

Sarah rinsed the sponge mop, wrung it, and then leaned it mopside up against the wall to dry. Whiskey eyed her from his throne, a leather chair in the waiting room. He knew they would leave after she pulled the last load of towels from the dryer and folded them. It was part of their routine in preparation for Monday.

"What should we do about dinner?" Sarah asked Whiskey. She knew Jared was picking up the supplies for tomorrow morning's baking marathon, but she hadn't really considered what they would eat for supper. "Chinese food?" Sarah asked the dog, who cocked his head and rotated his ear at the question.

"Mexican?" She folded a towel and added it to the stack near the wash tub that was against the back wall.

"Maybe burritos," she said, thinking aloud.

Whiskey climbed down from his perch and walked under the counter toward her just as someone wrapped their knuckles on the Coiffure's green locked door. Like a bullet from a low-caliber gun, Whiskey flew to the door, barking to let the intruder know he would rip them apart if given the command.

"Gees, dog," Sarah said, following after him. "You can clearly see through the glass that it's John Beams."

Sarah unlocked the door and opened it. "Hey, John."

He stepped inside and Whiskey rubbed up against the leg of his uniform. "Sarah. Whiskey." He scratched under Whiskey's chin.

"What's up?" Sarah asked.

"You know how Chief James put out a call for anyone who had footage of people entering or exiting the park to let us know?"

Sarah nodded her head.

"We were inundated. Apparently most people around have either those Ring cameras or cameras on the corners of their houses."

"Really? I wasn't expecting that here," Sarah admitted.

"Yeah, we didn't realize there were so many either. But we've been going through all of it, as tedious as it is." He pulled some black and white slightly grainy photos from a manilla envelope in his hand. "This is you and Whiskey," he said, pointing to what was clearly the back of a woman who was most likely Sarah and the fluffy tailed dog walking five feet in front and off to the right of her. The photo had a time stamp of five twenty-eight.

Officer Beams flipped to the next photo. "This is the person who walked into the park two minutes after you." The image was of someone wearing a knit beanie of an indeterminate color, a maybe black or charcoal gray puffy coat, what were probably jeans, and either hiking or work boots. It was difficult to tell as the quality wasn't great and the image had been taken at a distance. Sarah couldn't even tell if the person was male or female. No hair was visible. There were no distinguishing features.

"I didn't see that person," Sarah said.

"Take a good look. Notice the way the person walks, the way

their leg is bent."

"Yea, I see, but I don't know who that is."

"I don't either," John admitted. "But I'm hoping someone will. You and Whiskey were literally the last people to enter the park before this person. And we have footage from the other end of the park showing you exiting the park to walk down your street." John flipped to the third photo in the stack and showed her. The distance it was taken from was even further than the photos of her back. But if you knew Whiskey and knew her, you would probably recognize them.

"Do you have a photo like this of that person?"

John pulled out the fourth photo from the stack. "This wasn't from the same camera as that last image. This was from a different part of the park." This still showed an almost inch-worm sized person with no features, almost a dark gray blob, with the small glow of a tree on fire behind them.

"It's not much to work with," Sarah said. "But I see the tree is already burning by the time the person leaves."

"Yes. We used a magnifying glass and we think the person may have a ski mask pulled down over their face at that moment. But we aren't sure. The resolution is terrible. But does the build or the stance or walk or anything remind you of anyone you know or anyone you've seen?"

"No one comes to mind. I can't even tell if the person is average build or heavy because of the winter clothing. I mean, the legs in what I'm assuming are jeans, don't look skinny or stick like. But the jeans in that first photo you showed me don't look fitted. They are a baggier cut...like boyfriend jeans on a woman or regular cut jeans, as opposed to skinny or straight legged on a guy."

"What do you mean?" John had flipped back to the second photo he showed her.

Sarah pointed to the thigh area though it was still hard to discern anything about the person. "See here. It looks a little fuller through the thigh and tapers just slightly from the knee to the ground or the boots. It's not very clear, but I think it does that."

John squinted at the photo.

"Hang on," Sarah said. She pulled her phone from her back pocket and took a photo of the photograph. Then she pinched her fingers together on the screen and spread them apart to enlarge the image. She stared at the pants. "Look, you can sort of see it here." She pointed to what she was talking about. "But you're right. The resolution of this image is terrible."

"I know, but it is what we have to go on." John frowned.

"You guys or the fire inspector found nothing at the scene?"

"Only the accelerant."

Sarah pressed her lips tightly together and gave a slight shake of her head like she hated to hear that. Then she remembered the Trident wrapper. "Umm, the morning after the fire I found a gum wrapper lying on the ground not too far from the tree. I picked it up but figured it could have been from anyone, a firefighter, one of the bystanders or lookie-loos, you or one of the other officers, anyone."

"Do you still have it?"

"Yes, at home. I don't know why I didn't throw it away. It seems silly since it is probably nothing."

"Or it could be something. How about if I drive you and Whiskey home and you hand it over so we can process it. That's the only way we learn if it is something or nothing related to this case."

"Okay. I really wish I could help you more. Did you post these photos to the Cottageville message board or put them up in the library or Java and Juice or run them in the Courier, asking 'Do you know this person?'."

"Not yet. We planned that tomorrow if you didn't know who it was. In an hour's time frame before the fire, Sarah, only you and Whiskey, and this person went into the park and left before half of the town and the emergency services crews arrived because of the fire." John rubbed a hand over his brow and eyes.

"Only us?"

"Yes. It was a cold day and a very slow one for visits to the park."

Quietly Sarah said, "And I didn't see anyone."

"It may be safer for you that way." He grimaced at her.

"But it doesn't help you at all."

"We'll find the perpetrator, Sarah. You know we will. Now come on, if you're done here, let's go get that gum wrapper."

Sarah said to give her a minute so she could fold the rest of the towels. She turned down the thermostat and then slipped her arms into her jacket and zipped it up. The sun was starting to dip and so was the temperature.

On the way to their house, Whiskey rode in the backseat, behind the partition like a criminal, but he didn't seem to mind. "Are you working next Saturday or will you be marching in the parade with Coco Chanel and Braidington?" Sarah asked.

"I'm working it, but I may walk a block or two with them. We'll have to see how busy the department is that day. I never thought a corgi would steal my heart. I'm a big dog guy." He rumbled with a deep laugh.

"There are worse animals to have as part of a partner package deal." Sarah grinned at him.

"True. Those hairless breeds creep me out."

Sarah cracked up. "Said the big, bad cop."

He shrugged. "Everyone's got something..." John pulled his black and white car into Sarah's driveway and killed the engine. He opened the back door, and Whiskey jumped from the seat and made a pit stop at a rhododendron near the front of the house.

Sarah opened the door and told John to come on in, that she wouldn't be a minute. She left him standing in the entryway while she raced off to her room to pull the wrapper from her nightstand, which is where she put it for safekeeping. As she reached inside the drawer, she thought better of grabbing it with her bare hands so she picked up a tissue and used that to extract it. She carried it inside the tissue to John and handed it over, and he enclosed it in a small evidence bag and sealed it shut.

"Thank you, Sarah. I appreciate your help."

"Is it okay if I show Jared and my friends the photo I took with my phone to see if they know anything?"

"Yes, absolutely. And we are looking forward to seeing you at the surprise party tomorrow. Can we bring anything?"

"No. We have it all taken care of. But thanks."

"No problem. If that changes, give me a call or text."

"Sounds good."

As Sarah opened the door and started to walk John out, she saw Jared driving down her street. She waved her hand to get his attention and held up one finger to signal for him to wait one minute for John to back out of the driveway.

"Have a great night, Sarah," John said, getting into his car.

"You too," Sarah said though she didn't think he heard her as he had shut his door.

Sarah shuffled from foot to foot as Officer Beams drove off and Jared arrived, pulling two bags of groceries from his passenger seat. "Give me one of those," Sarah said, taking a paper sack from him and kissing him lightly on the stubble on his cheek.

"Mi'lady," Jared said, "sustenance has arrived."

"Ugh!" Sarah exclaimed. "I meant to stop for burritos on the way home, but then John stopped by and..." Her voice trailed off, wondering what she had in the freezer that she could quick-thaw for supper.

"Great minds think alike, my love," Jared's eyes sparkled as he reached back into his vehicle and pulled out a sack of food from their favorite taqueria.

"Just one more reason I love you," Sarah said, leading the way back into her house.

CHAPTER NINE

At two-thirty Sunday afternoon, Sarah parked the CJ in front of Ginger's house. She wore a forest green sweater dress and knee-high dark brown leather boots under her winter coat. She had adorned Whiskey with a heart bandana for the occasion, since he had been the only dog invited to celebrate Daniel and Ginger's engagement. She and Jared just needed to keep him quiet and out of sight until everyone yelled "Surprise."

Jared had chosen jeans of the deepest blue, a forest green t-shirt, and a brown and forest green tweed sports coat—which he wore under a topcoat since it was too cold for a blazer alone—along with brown Chelsea boots, to coordinate with Sarah, even though she said it wasn't necessary. She wasn't a fan of when couples went all matchy-matchy.

Jared and Whiskey climbed out of the Jeep while Sarah punched in the numbered code to unlock the front door. Whiskey explored a trail of scent that wrapped around the side of the farmhouse. His wriggling nose was to the ground, and his tail swished back and forth like a broom without anything to sweep since the yard was devoid of leaves or snow.

The door beeped and the deadbolt and bottom lock disengaged so Sarah depressed the metal lever above the handle and pushed open the big wooden door. She lugged a tote bag filled with decorations toward the kitchen and knew that Jared would follow her with the boxes of cupcakes. They left the front door open as they walked back and forth unloading the car until it was empty of all of the party supplies. On their last trip in, with the balloon bouquet, Whiskey followed them into the living room, where Jared anchored the balloon bouquet to the circular handle of the copper firewood tub that sat on the hearth of the majestic stone fireplace, the focal point of one wall. He made sure the ribbons were tied tightly to the handle as he didn't want the balloons taking off for the vaulted ceiling where no one would get to them again until they ran out of helium and floated back to earth.

"I think if we build a fire, those balloons can't stay there," Sarah said, eying the red mylar hearts and the gold confetti latex orbs.

"We can't build a fire until after they get here," Jared said. "The smoke would be a dead giveaway that someone was in their home."

Sarah chuckled. "Would definitely ruin the surprise. I didn't think of that."

"If you give me your keys, I'll drive the Jeep to that spot at the back of their property off the dirt road. That way we don't have to worry about it later." Sarah had made it clear to everyone who was coming to the party that they had to park at the back of the five acres so the vehicles wouldn't be seen from the house. Originally, she had thought that maybe people could park behind the big red barn like Daniel suggested, but when she and Whiskey had eaten chili with Ginger a few days ago, she realized the back end of the barn and the ground behind was visible as she drove up the long driveway.

While Jared took care of the car, Sarah got out the step ladder from a tall cupboard near the back door so she could hang a banner above the dining room table. Since the cupcakes already spelled out congratulations, the banner featured two filled champagne glasses tilted toward each other and the words "Cheers to the happy couple." She used twine to attach the corners of the vinyl banner to the frame of the wooden and wrought iron light fixture that hung centered over the table.

Then she returned to the kitchen to pick up one of the two rustic but colorful centerpieces in wooden boxes she had made from the local shop, Blooms and Bouquets, and set that on a blue runner in the middle of the big maple dining table. Sarah planned to put in this room the boxes of pizza and the two bowls of green salad, along with the white paper plates emblazoned in black with "love" in script and a small red heart as if it were accenting the e, the matching napkins, and the eco-friendly cutlery.

The other centerpiece Sarah carried from the kitchen into the living room, which was more like a great room in size and flow, and she set that one in the middle of a big square wooden coffee table that was boxed in on three sides by sumptuous, tan leather sofas. Sarah draped a second banner in front of the fireplace mantel and placed the marble candle holder pillars that were already there atop the banner's edge to anchor it. This banner read, "You're engaged has a nice ring to it!"

Just as Sarah had the banner secured and hanging as she wanted it, Whiskey barked once and ran to the front door. Jared had returned from moving the Jeep. "Hey, Sarah," he called. "I know it is cold out and their garage is probably not insulated, but we should probably put those bottles of champagne in the fridge or wine cooler to ensure they are the right temperature for drinking."

"Oh, good thinking." Sarah pulled her boots back on that she had left by the front door, but left her coat in the kitchen, and headed back outside to the detached garage with Jared. They found half a dozen bottles exactly where Daniel said he had left them, so they each grabbed two, thinking four bottles should be plenty.

They added those to the kitchen's wine cooler since the refrigerator already held the salads, the five six-packs of bottled beer, three two-liter bottles of soda, and the three bottles of white wine that they had brought for the party. Three bottles of red wine sat on the kitchen counter, next to cake plates that matched the bigger love plates that were now in the dining room.

"What else do we need to do?" Jared asked.

"Let's get the glassware from the cupboard and set it on the kitchen bartop." Glassware was the only concession Sarah made to the otherwise disposable or compostable items. She wanted easy clean up, but she refused to drink champagne or wine from a plastic cup and knew Ginger hated that, too. Jared grabbed half a dozen wine glasses—a mixture of shapes to best serve both whites and reds, two pilsner glasses and two beer mugs—though he expected most of the beer drinkers would consume straight from the bottles, and some glasses for soft drinks or water. Sarah pulled ten crystal champagne glasses from a cabinet in Ginger and Daniel's dining room. She carried them carefully, one in each hand, to the kitchen, making multiple trips until they all stood reflecting the overhead recessed lights over the bar.

The sound of a ringing handbell echoed through the house, and Whiskey ran toward the front door barking like a drill sergeant giving orders at full volume. "Quiet down, please," Sarah yelled as she raced to answer the door. It was, as she expected, the pizzas being delivered.

Josh, the teenaged delivery driver, was hidden behind the height of the stack of six boxes of large pies.

"Hey, Josh," Jared said, pulling the pizzas from the seventeen-year-old's arms. "I'm impressed you carried them all in one go."

Josh's eyes sparkled at the compliment. "Jared, you know it's how I work out," he joked.

"It's better than lifting pizza to your mouth." Jared slapped Josh lightly on the arm. "Good to see you. You crushed it this week." Josh was part of Jared's gaming group, and Sarah had heard the stories that Josh took all of the games they played seriously and was working at the pizzeria to save money for college. He was determined to study game design as his major. In his spare time, Jared coached Josh in increasing his drawing skills.

After they said goodbye and watched Josh do a three-point turn to go down the driveway, Jared took the pizzas into the kitchen, turned the oven on warm, and put the boxes into the oven. Sarah was grateful Ginger's ovens were commercial grade, otherwise all six boxes wouldn't have fit.

The final thing she and Jared did was to put some crudites on a fancy bamboo cutting board. Little bowls dotted the board, each bowl holding a separate item: green olives, black olives, pepperoncini, roasted red peppers, cashews, almonds, walnuts, and pecans. And piled at the very end of the board were quick-pickled veggies: cucumbers, asparagus, green beans, and baby carrots that Jared had made a week ago. They carried this board into the dining room just as the first guest walked through the back door. Whiskey did his job running to greet the newcomers, but he didn't bark since he immediately recognized Emily, Travis, and Taylor.

Emily and Taylor were in their usual all-black attire. Emily wore a black minidress, black tights, and her combat boots. But on the occasion of celebrating love, and so close to Valentine's Day, she had bleached her hair blonde and dyed a red heart-shaped patch on the side of her head above her ear.

"That looks so cool," Jared exclaimed when she took off her beanie to reveal the new design.

Emily beamed at him. "Thank you. I did it last night."

Travis grabbed ahold of Emily's hand and squeezed it, smiling at her. "I helped," he said.

"He sure did," Emily said. "I couldn't hold the stencil and paint the dye at the same time."

Taylor stared at the ground and shuffled his feet and looked uncomfortable, so Sarah asked, "How's school and work going, Taylor?"

His eyes met hers and he mumbled, "Okay."

"Learning anything new?" Sarah prodded.

"Some." Taylor stuck a finger under the collar of his black denim button down shirt and scratched his neck.

"Want to take off your coats?" Sarah asked.

"Follow me," Jared said. He showed them the downstairs guest room where they were stashing the winter coats and whatever else people didn't want to hold onto for the evening, and then he gave them a quick tour of the house. None of the three had been there before.

While they were upstairs, the back door opened again and Sarah welcomed Candace Grimes, who had ridden with her police department colleague John Beams and his partner Braidington Bagley. Candace looked stunning in a red velvet knee-length dress, and Sarah realized it was one of the very few times she had seen her friend forgo pants for something more festive. Braidington always looked like he could be featured on the cover of GQ, and this afternoon was no different. He looked impeccable in black jeans with black biker boots, and a red quarter-zip cashmere sweater. A black cashmere scarf hung casually around his neck under his thick leather moto jacket. Sarah was in awe of his cheekbones and sparkling eyes every time she admired the attractive lawyer. He reminded her of actor Jharrel

Jerome with his cafe au lait skin and almost blinding wide smile. And since John and Braidington had started spending time together, Sarah noticed that John seemed to care more about his clothing choices. He wore gray cords with black boots and a blue and white horizontal striped wool sweater with just the peek of a white crew neck t-shirt showing at the neckline, like he had stepped from the pages of an L.L. Bean catalogue.

Braidington carried a foot-long square box wrapped in silver and white paper and tied with a silver bow. "I know you said no gifts, Sarah," he said, "but it seemed poor etiquette to not get them a housewarming present at the very least. Where would you like me to put it?"

"The kitchen counter is good." She, too, didn't heed the no gift rule. Sarah had ordered two cut-crystal champagne glasses that she figured Ginger and Daniel could use the day of their wedding at the reception. That gift was wrapped and sitting on the kitchen counter abutting the refrigerator so it would be out of the way.

When Jared, Emily, Travis, Taylor, and Whiskey returned down the stairs, Sarah asked Jared to give the latest arrivers the tour, while she took their winter coats and put them in the spare bedroom. And when that tour was over, she made sure everyone had a drink in their hands, and then she turned out the lights all over the house. They all crowded into the dining room to graze on the appetizers by the fading sunlight and to await the arrival of Daniel and Ginger. At ten minutes to four, they heard Ginger's SUV pull up the driveway. Sarah had Whiskey by the collar and Jared was holding his mouth shut and quietly saying, "Shhh," to him.

Moments passed that felt long and tense, like a spring about to pop.

Finally, Sarah heard the familiar beeps from the electronic keypad and the clicks of the locks disengaging. Everyone in the dining room seemed to be holding their breath, except for Whiskey who tried to wriggle himself free from Sarah's hold.

A light turned on in the house's foyer, and a closet door opened.

"Thank you for such a special day," Ginger said, followed by a smack of her lips on Daniel's, the sound of which caused Sarah to smile to herself.

Daniel and Ginger's footsteps echoed as they walked across the slate floor of the entryway. Soon they would pass the dining room where everyone stood as still as marble statues.

But Whiskey couldn't take the tension any longer. He let out a yip and broke away from Sarah like a stallion shaking off its reins. The whole room went with it, and yelled, "Surprise!" And John Beams turned on the dining room lights.

"Oh my!" Ginger exclaimed, eying her friends. "Wait?! Did you do this?" she asked her fiancé.

A grin lit Daniel's face like a three-wick candle. A picnic basket hung from one of his hands and he held a colorful Mexican blanket in his other arm.

"And you," Ginger said, pointing at Sarah. "You kept this a secret."

"I did," Sarah said, giving her BFF a hug. "We wanted to celebrate your big day. You did say yes, right?" She inspected Ginger's left hand and found her fourth finger empty. Sarah frowned. When her eyes searched Ginger's, distress like an S.O.S. signal broadcast from Sarah's face.

"You know I don't wear rings, silly," Ginger said, pulling from beneath her sweater a platinum chain that was secured around her neck. On the chain was a platinum round diamond solitaire engagement ring.

Daniel said, "I knew she couldn't make all of that bread and stuff while wearing a ring on her finger, and I didn't want to buy something she had to keep taking on and off and remember where she put it. So I crafted another way for it to work." Love poured from his eyes as he gazed at his fiancée.

"Smart man," Ginger said, leaning close to him to kiss him again.

Murmurs of agreement punctuated the room.

"We need to toast the happy couple, so I'll go get the champagne," Jared said. He moved from the dining room to the kitchen, turning on lights as he went and pulled two bottles of bubbly from the wine fridge. Candace trailed him to help.

Five minutes later, everyone in the house was standing in a loose circle and was holding aloft a glass of finely bubbled beverage. "As you know," Jared said, "this group right here loves to celebrate anything. And I mean *anything*."

Chuckles answered his comment.

"But I can't think of a better reason to raise a glass today than to honor the love and commitment of Daniel and Ginger. They are resilient and kind and two of the best damn people I know in a town full of fine people. Congratulations on your engagement. We love you."

Whiskey, who had been standing at attention near Jared's feet, gave a "woof" of approval.

"Here, here," said John and Braidington.

"What he said," said Sarah, clinking her glass against Jared's before working her way around the circle.

"Thank you, all of you," Ginger said.

"Now tell us all about how he proposed," Emily requested.

"Let's hear it over food," Sarah said. "We'll be right back with it." She and Jared, followed by Travis and Taylor, who said they would help, went into the kitchen and pulled the pizzas from the oven and turned the dial from warm to off. "That's a lot of pizza," Taylor said, his eyes bugging at the six large boxes.

"We wouldn't want anyone to leave hungry," Sarah said, handing each one of the T's a bowl of salad and serving utensils to go with them. "Please take those in the dining room. We've got the pizzas."

As they re-entered the dining room, Emily said, "Oh, that smells so good."

"Everyone," Sarah said, "the pizzas, salads, and crudites are in here. The drinks are in the kitchen, as well as cupcakes and small plates for dessert. I figured most people would like to eat in the big living room, if that's okay with Ginger and Daniel, as we can be more relaxed that way." Sarah looked at Ginger and Daniel for confirmation on dining in the great room.

"I'll get a fire going in there." Daniel headed in that direction.

Ten minutes later, Whiskey was stretched out and half-asleep in front of the hearth. All ten friends had their drinks refreshed and their plates filled with food, and they settled on the leather sofas and chairs around the big coffee table. The fire was roaring and the balloons had been moved to the dining room to keep them from deflating or popping from the heat.

Ginger raved about the elegant decorations and festive plates while she ate a slice of mushroom and pepperoni pizza. She and Daniel tag teamed the telling of the story of their picnic and what he said as he proposed. And Ginger admitted her surprise and that she cried when the feeling of love for him was so strong she realized that yes, she did indeed want to get married. And how happy she was that he wanted to go down that path again and with her.

Sarah caught Jared's eye at that statement, and she gave him a half-smile as if to say, "Isn't love grand? It helps heal and creates new memories."

In response, he blew her a kiss, which made her smile and made her heart feel even fuller than it had so far this evening celebrating love with the people she loved. She sighed. Life really was incredible sometimes; it felt like a warm blanket wrapping you snug. Contentment filled Sarah as she sipped her wine and talked with her friends.

CHAPTER TEN

But that contentment deflated the next morning as if a big bird beak pierced Sarah's bubble of peace. The day started like many other days. Sarah awoke at five-thirty without an alarm. She let Whiskey out to do his business and then fed him; took a quick shower; donned the day's almost-uniform of jeans, a t-shirt, and a sweatshirt with "easily distracted by dogs" printed on the front of it; and then put on her winter gear to go for a walk.

The sky was steely gray and the forecast called for flurries so Sarah and Whiskey walked quickly up their street to the park. It was as if the dog knew Sarah was too cold for him to sniff every blade of grass and every plant or animal burrow he stumbled across that morning. Instead, he trotted in a straight line, occasionally glancing over his right shoulder to ensure she was following him. At the park entrance, he sat on his haunches and waited for her to catch up.

"Good boy," she said when she was within reach to scratch his ears.

Inside the park, Whiskey led Sarah to the scorched tree. He sniffed around its base, nose to the ground, jockeying left and right and then circling before jutting one direction and circling again. He reminded Sarah of a compass that was affected too strongly by the earth's magnetic field so it spun.

"What do you smell?" Sarah's breath plumed white with each word. She knew he couldn't answer, but she asked the question just the same.

He cocked one ear toward her and gave her a side-eye glance.

Eventually, he gave up or caught the trail of something else because he was suddenly racing toward the empty children's playground. Sarah scurried after him, but she couldn't see what was causing his excitement. The ring of Sarah's cell phone punctured the still air, and Sarah pulled it out of her puffy jacket pocket and glanced at the screen.

"Hey, Ginger," she answered.

"Are you out walking Whiskey?"

"Yes. What's up?"

"Come to the cafe right now."

"Umm okay. Is everything alright?"

"Yes. No. I'll tell you when you get here." With that, Ginger hung up.

Weird, Sarah thought. Java and Juice wouldn't be open for another fifteen minutes. "Come on, Whiskey, we need to go see Ginger." She waited for him to join her and then together, they walked to the Main Street park exit and entrance. The walk sign was on when they got to the sidewalk so they crossed Main Street and waved at Bill on his porch from the far side of the street. "We'll stop on the way back," Sarah yelled, hoping he heard her.

Half a block down on the right was Java and Juice's welcoming red door. Sarah was surprised to find Ginger standing on the other side of it, awaiting her arrival. Her friend's face looked pale and her eyes were lined with worry.

"What's wrong?" Sarah asked when she and Whiskey were inside the cafe and Ginger had locked the door behind them.

Sarah heard noises coming from behind the swinging doors that led to the kitchen and figured Jared or Jared and Taylor were finishing the pastries for the day.

"My necklace is gone." Tears spilled from Ginger's eyes.

"Your engagement necklace?" Sarah eyed Ginger's neck, but she couldn't tell if the platinum chain and ring were hiding under Ginger's apron and sweater.

Ginger wiped her eyes with her fingers, smearing her mascara. She sniffed noisily. "No. The antique one."

"Wait. What? You mean the one you showed me last week?"

"Yes, the diamond and sapphire one." Ginger sniffed again.

"What do you mean by it is gone?"

"It isn't there in the drawer in my bedroom any more."

"Did you take it out and show it to anyone besides me lately?

Could it have been accidentally put into a different drawer or not put away?"

Ginger shook her head no which caused her high ponytail to swish.

"And Daniel didn't take it to be professionally cleaned or anything? Maybe as a surprise to you?"

"I don't think so. He didn't say that."

"So he knows it wasn't where you had been keeping it?"

Ginger nodded her head. "I told him this morning right before we both left for work."

"And what did he say?"

"That it had to be there somewhere and that we'd look for it tonight. But I already did, Sarah. I was late this morning because I was tearing our room apart. And I feel sick. Just sick. When we called his parents on the way home from the park to tell them we got engaged, his mom went on and on about how happy it would make her for me to wear the necklace as my something old and something blue for our wedding. And now I don't know where it is." Ginger's tears fell afresh.

"It couldn't have just disappeared," Sarah said. "It's got to be somewhere. I'll come over after work today and help you look. I'm sure we'll find it somewhere silly. Like you meant to put it in the drawer but instead you put the frozen peas in your drawer and the necklace is in the freezer or something like that." Even though she was trying to lighten the situation and make her BFF feel better and have hope, Sarah wondered if it was possible that someone broke in and stole the necklace. She frowned.

"Hey, Ginger, umm, you haven't had any workers in your house since we ate chili, have you? I mean the construction has been finished, right?"

Ginger's shiny blue eyes widened. "You think someone could have stolen it?"

Sarah shrugged. "Are you missing anything else?"

"I don't think so. Or I haven't noticed anything. But no one has been working in our house for more than two weeks. The only people who have been in our house since you were there with Whiskey..."

The dog's ears perked up at the sound of his name.

"...was everyone who was at the party last night." Ginger pursed her lips and narrowed her eyes. And then she ticked off on her fingers, "Two cops, my two employees, your employee and her boyfriend, a lawyer, and you. It's highly unlikely any of you would steal anything at all let alone from me."

"I agree," Sarah said. "Plus I don't remember anyone but you and Daniel going up your stairs by yourselves at any time during the festivities."

"Me neither," Ginger said, "but someone could have used a bathroom if the downstairs one was occupied."

"True. But let's work from the assumption that the necklace has been misplaced. Was the velvet box in the drawer or was the box and the necklace not there?"

"Nothing was there. Just the stack of t-shirts I keep atop the box and necklace."

"Hmm. Well, like I said, I'll come over after work today and help you look. We'll figure out what happened. Okay?"

Ginger wiped her eyes again. "Okay."

Sarah gave her a hug and said quietly, "I love you. But Ging, you may want to pop into the bathroom. You have a slight raccoon situation because of the tears."

"Oh no," Ginger said, power walking toward the powder room in the public area of the cafe. "Thanks," she called over her shoulder. "You always have my back."

"Of course I do," Sarah said. "Whiskey and I will be back in an hour with my tumbler and to pick up breakfast and lunch. Are you going to be okay?"

Through the bathroom door, Ginger said, "Yes. Thanks for coming here and providing comfort."

"Anytime."

Jared pushed through the swinging doors into the cafe. His lean arm muscles taut in his short sleeve shirt, he carried two huge silver trays of scones. "Oh hey, Sarah." Whiskey raced to greet him. "Down boy. I don't have free hands." Jared grinned and then tilted his head in the direction of the bathroom door. "Is she going to be okay?"

Sarah walked toward the front counter so she was closer to Jared. "Yes," Sarah said. "I'll go to her place after work and we'll find the necklace."

Jared put down the trays atop the glass case and then moved to the counter. "I hope you do. I haven't seen it, but she told me all about it and it sounds very special."

"It's exquisite. Anyway, it's good seeing you, as always. I'll be back in a bit with my tumbler."

They met halfway across the counter and kissed goodbye.

Ginger came out of the bathroom and the skin around her eyes had been scrubbed pink. "Thank you for coming when I called."

"Of course," Sarah said. "Focus on work and maybe your subconscious will whisper where the necklace is, if it got misplaced."

"Maybe. But I'm having problems believing I misplaced it."

"We'll figure it out," Sarah reiterated. "Bye for now. Come on, Whiskey." They left the cafe and crossed Main Street, stopping by Bill's to snag Whiskey a treat, but they didn't stay and chat as he was on a call and they really didn't have the time. They jogged through the park and down their street, Whiskey beating Sarah to their front door, her breathing fast and heavy in the cold air.

Sarah fixed her hair and then grabbed her empty to-go coffee cup, some dinner for Whiskey in case they ran late at Ginger's, her backpack containing her laptop, and her purse and car keys. She'd need her Jeep to get to Ginger's later. "Come on, Whisk. We are driving to work today. Hop in." She held the door open for him and he jumped onto her seat and then into the passenger seat. Sometimes he liked to ride shotgun as opposed to sitting in the back like Sarah was his chauffeur.

Sarah bypassed Java and Juice as no parking was available in front of it and drove to the Coiffure. Emily was already inside with the lights on, so Sarah unlocked the door and let Whiskey inside. "Hey, Em. I'm headed to Java and Juice to get coffee and our breakfast and lunch. Do you need a coffee, too?"

Emily picked up her tumbler and drank whatever was in it and handed the empty cup to Sarah. "I do now." She grinned.

"Black or are you going fancy today?"

"Black like my wardrobe." Em snorted.

"Nice. Any other requests?"

"If they have those chocolate chunk scones with the cinnamon hearts..." Emily's voice trailed off.

"I'm sure they will. They are the holiday special."

"Speaking of holiday specials, I was looking over our schedule today. Does it really say Prissy is coming in for a dye job? I didn't know we did that." Emily's eyebrows were raised and curiosity danced across her face like a cat watching a feather toy, eager and slightly incredulous.

"Yes. I ran into Peg on Main Street and she went on and on about how she wanted to dye the poor poodle pink for Valentine's Day. But you know Peg, right?"

Emily said, "Yeah, but mostly of her. I don't really know her personally."

"Well, let's just say she's often messy, and she's been known to do things without thinking of the consequences. And sometimes those consequences have been, um, dangerous."

Emily's eyes widened. "Dangerous," she repeated.

"Yeah, so when she said she was going to dye the dog I figured we should intervene. I could just see her poisoning Prissy by mistake or using something permanent or toxic. That's why I got this dye." Sarah pulled a jar of temporary critter color in red out of her backpack. "And said we'd take care of dying her ears and tail."

"Oooo, can I do it, Sarah? I want to do it." Emily's enthusiasm oozed from her.

"Of course you can. After I saw last night the way your hair looked, how perfect and festive, I figured you'd be the ideal person to make Peg's dream come true...even without Travis to help you this time."

"Thanks, Sarah, and you know, this could start a trend of a new service we can offer."

"Umm, yeah, about that. I don't really want to encourage people to dye their pets."

"I agree that it isn't the best idea. And most of our human clients probably wouldn't be interested anyway, but I'm sure an occasional one would, like those people who paint their dog's toenails."

Sarah smiled at her assistant. "Yeah, I'm not a fan of that either. But to each their own as long as their pet is treated well and is safe. Okay. I'm off to Java and Juice. I'll be back in a few minutes. I'm leaving Whiskey with you."

When Sarah got to Java and Juice, she found the place buzzing with energy and people. Most of the tables were full, and many people said hello to Sarah as she passed by them on her way to the counter. Ginger's game face was engaged as she joked with her patrons, frothed milk and made foam art in freshly poured drinks, and plated her flaky, delicate delicacies. It warmed Sarah's heart to see her best friend enjoying the morning instead of ruminating on the missing necklace.

She handed Jared both tumblers and he remarked, "You doublefisting your caffeine fix, mi'lady?"

"One is Em's."

"Ah. Black too?"

"She said black like her wardrobe."

Jared smirked. "At least she didn't say like her soul."

"Too cliche. Two of those special scones with the cinnamon hearts you brought out earlier. Is barbeque chicken on the salad menu today?"

"It is indeed." Jared put two scones and two salads in a bag, and handed the two tumblers to Sarah after she tapped her card against the reader. "Can you carry all of that?"

"Yes. I'm good. Thank you." She puckered her lips at him and made a kissing sound and then turned and walked toward the door, thankful that someone was entering just as she needed to exit, as she did not have a hand free to open the door.

Chief James held the door for her and said "Sarah, I heard you hosted a shindig that now has two of my deputies mainlining coffee this morning."

Sarah smiled. "I don't think that's my fault. It was an early night since Ginger is an early riser."

"I'm joking. But I am looking forward to congratulating the happy couple. Plus, I want to put more of these flyers in the cafe." Chief James showed Sarah the image on the top paper in his hand: an enlargement of the person leaving the park. The resolution wasn't any clearer but the details still led Sarah to think the jeans were on the baggy side. She squinted her eyes searching for the shape of a label on the jacket, but came up empty. It was taken from too far away to get any details.

"No luck yet and no leads?" Sarah asked.

"Nothing substantial. Have a good day, Sarah."

"You, too, Chief. And I'm keeping my eyes open, mostly for that silhouette." She tilted her head toward the paper in his hand.

CHAPTER ELEVEN

Nine hours later, Ginger's farmhouse was quiet, except for the soft creak of floorboards under Sarah's boots and the rhythmic tapping of Whiskey's nails against the polished wood. The air carried the faint scent of last night's pizza and roses from the arrangements Sarah had put in the dining and living rooms, mingling with the earthy aroma of the fire smoldering in the stone fireplace. Sarah glanced at Ginger, who stood in the middle of her bedroom with her arms crossed, worry etched into her face. Other than Ginger's anxiety, the room was a serene space with soft gray walls, white bedding, and a large bay window that overlooked the backyard and fields beyond. "I swear, I had it right here," Ginger said, pointing to the top drawer of her dresser. The drawer had been pulled open and displayed two neat stacks of folded t-shirts.

Whiskey sniffed the air, his ears perking up as if he sensed the tension in the room. Sarah gave him a pat on the head. "All right, boy, let's see if you can help us out."

"What if someone stole it?" Ginger's voice quivered.

"Let's not jump to conclusions," Sarah said. "We'll check the house first. Maybe it slipped under something or got knocked behind the dresser. You were tired when you showed it to me last week. It could've ended up anywhere."

Ginger nodded reluctantly. "Where do you think we should start?"

"Maybe let me search your dresser, drawer by drawer, and for that matter, maybe after I search each drawer I take it out and look behind it. Maybe the box was accidentally put atop the shirts instead of under them and then fell back behind the drawer when you opened it."

"I doubt it..." Ginger started, before Sarah cut her off with, "Probably not, but what do we have to lose by being thorough in our search."

Whiskey darted around the room, sniffing near the bed, the dresser, and the plush armchair in the corner. Then he circled back to the bed. He pawed at the quilt and let out a soft whine.

"What is it, boy?" Sarah asked, lifting the corner of the quilt. Whiskey dove under the bed, his tail wagging furiously. A moment later, he emerged, carrying a stray sock in his mouth.

Ginger let out a shaky laugh. "Not quite the treasure we're

looking for, but thanks, Whiskey. I'll make sure Daniel gets that back so he'll have a pair."

"Maybe you could search your nightstands, while I look in the dresser." Sarah and Ginger shared almost everything, but she also knew nightstands often contained more personal products than dressers. She didn't really want to get that intimate with the love lives of her friends.

"Okay," Ginger agreed.

Sarah removed one stack of t-shirts from the top drawer and looked under each shirt one by one. Then she did the same for the other stack of shirts. Ginger was correct. The velvet box with the necklace wasn't there, nor was the necklace hidden among the folds.

She pulled the whole drawer out of the dresser and looked down to the drawer below. No necklace. She frowned, reinserted the drawer, and stacked the t-shirts back into it and shut it, and then moved on to drawer two and repeated the whole routine.

By the time she finished the dresser, Sarah was a tiny bit frustrated. She really had expected that the necklace and its box had been misplaced into one of the other drawers. She moved on to the second dresser in the bedroom, while Ginger emptied the second nightstand in the room onto the bed and then methodically refilled it.

"Do you have a polishing cloth or anything else from the relative who owned the necklace before you?" Sarah asked. "I know Whiskey isn't a bloodhound, but when we were looking for Mrs. Jenkins, he proved adept at following a scent trail."

Ginger's mouth was downturned as she said, "No, I don't."

"Okay. We'll just keep looking. Help me lift the corner of your mattress so we can check between it and the frame."

"Umm, I'm sure I didn't it put it there."

"I don't believe you did either. But I will leave no place unsearched."

Ginger and Sarah as a team lifted one side of the mattress and then the other. The only thing they found was a dust bunny.

"Let's tackle your closet next."

The walk-in closet was a meticulously organized space with a his-side and a her-side. On both sides the clothes were arranged by color and by type. Shirts together. Jeans together. Pants together. Ginger's collection of shoes lined the floor on her side, each pair neatly placed in its designated spot. Daniel's six pairs of shoes sat under two suits and three pairs of dress pants. Whiskey sniffed around the baseboards, occasionally pausing to investigate a stray shoelace or the hem of a coat.

In order to be thorough, Sarah stuck her hand in every pocket she found. She climbed a step stool and checked the top shelves, but there was no sign of the necklace. "Nothing here. Let's move on."

The search continued through the rest of the house. They combed through the upstairs guest room, the office, the cushions of the leather sofas in the living room, and even the laundry room. Whiskey's enthusiasm never wavered, though his discoveries—a crumpled receipt, his own plush toy he had lost under a wingback chair on a prior visit, and a lint covered sock that had slid between the clothes dryer and washer—did little to further their progress.

By the time they reached the kitchen, Ginger was visibly distraught. "What if it really was stolen?" she said, leaning against the counter. "I should've been more careful."

Sarah placed a reassuring hand on her friend's shoulder. "We're not giving up yet. Let's think this through. Did you go anywhere else in the house the night you showed me the necklace? Let's walk through the time from when we left to when you went to bed."

Ginger frowned, trying to remember. "You guys left and Daniel still wasn't home. I decided I would read a little but was chilled. So I made a cup of herbal tea. And I think I stopped by the mudroom to grab a sweater, before taking the tea into the living room and lighting the fire. That's it."

"Then that's where we'll look next," Sarah said.

Whiskey seemed to agree, trotting toward the mudroom with renewed purpose. Sarah and Ginger followed him into the small, utilitarian space at the back of the house, where coats hung on hooks and boots lined the floor. Whiskey's nose went straight to a wicker basket on the shelf.

"What's in there?" Sarah asked.

Ginger pulled the basket down and began sifting through its contents. "Just some gloves, scarves, and hats. I don't see—wait, what's this?" She held up a delicate chain tangled around the fringe of a scarf. For a moment, hope sparked in her eyes, but it quickly faded. "It's just a bracelet."

Sarah's brow furrowed. "Well, at least we're on the right track. Let's check the living room again. Maybe you set it on a shelf or something when you were in there."

They checked the bookshelf and the drawer in the big coffee table. They even looked under the sofas this time by Sarah lifting an end and Ginger crouching to inspect the floor and underside of the sofas. But again, they only found dust bunnies and some old shards of potato chips.

"I'm getting a little embarrassed by our cleaning skills," Ginger said. "I thought our house was spotless."

Sarah chuckled. "No one's house is spotless. I think we all have crumbs in our couches and dirt trapped in our carpets and rugs. It's inevitable. I think the only rooms we haven't checked are the downstairs guest room and powder room, the kitchen, and the dining room. Oh and your front entry closet and garage."

"Only, huh? That sounds like a lot."

On their way to the guest bedroom, they heard the back door to the house open and Whiskey left them to go greet the intruder. He barked in warning as he bolted to the door.

"Hey, Whiskey," Sarah heard Daniel say. "You smelled the food, didn't you?"

"I asked him to stop at that Chinese place on his way home. I figured we'd work up an appetite with all of the searching."

"Good plan," Sarah said. She picked up the end of the comforter and peered under it to the bedding below. No lumps or anything shaped like a box. But she ran her hands over the sheets to double check and looked inside the pillowcases, before she and Ginger lifted the mattress and looked under the bed itself.

Sarah looked in the guest room nightstand while Ginger went through the chest of drawers.

Daniel popped his head into the room, with Whiskey by his side. "There you are. How's it going?"

"Found more things than I wanted to... but no necklace or blue velvet box."

Whiskey trotted to an old flowered couch that was crammed against a wall underneath two windows. He sniffed the cushions and then hopped onto the sofa and followed his nose along the top of the back. At one point he stopped and tried to jam his head between the wall and the sofa at about the midway point. When that didn't work, he pawed at the top of the sofa, like he was trying to get it to move.

"What is it, Whisk?" Sarah asked, joining him in the space. She peered with one eye into the sliver of space between the wall and sofa. "I can't really see anything," she remarked to no one in particular.

"Stand up," Daniel said. "And I'll pull it out."

Sarah climbed off the sofa. Daniel pulled it back by its bottom leg. When it was a couple of inches away from the wall, Whiskey wedged himself into the space, his tail wagging furiously.

"Oh my God, dog," Ginger said. "You're going to get stuck."

"Daniel pull it out more, please," Sarah said.

"Won't he drop? I don't want him to get hurt."

"He won't."

Whiskey gave a sharp yip of agreement, and Daniel slowly pulled the sofa back a few more inches, which allowed Whiskey to wiggle his way closer to the ground. Daniel pulled back another inch or two, and Whiskey reached the floor.

"Did you find something?" Sarah asked, peering over the back of the couch.

Whiskey emerged from the back of the couch triumphantly, a shiny object in his mouth.

Ginger gasped. "Is that it?"

Sarah took the object from Whiskey and held it up to the light. Her excitement faded as she realized what it was. "It's just a keychain."

Ginger groaned. "I don't understand. Whose keychain is that? And how did it get there? And where in the hell is the necklace?"

"Why don't we take a break?" Daniel asked. "Let's eat the sweet and sour pork and Kung Pao chicken while it is still warm. We can finish looking in the last few places when we are done."

Whiskey's tail swished back and forth like a metronome set to the tempo of happiness, as if saying, "Yes. Food. Yes. Food. Right now. Food."

Sarah laughed at him. "He's always up for a meal."

They ate at the kitchen bar amidst companionable chatting about their days and sharing customer drama. Sarah shared photos of the outstanding dye job Emily had done on Prissy. Instead of only coloring the white poodle's tail and ears red, Emily surprised Peg by handing over a heartfelt design job of red ears and tail plus a hand drawn, filled in red heart on the center of the poodle's back. Peg was so excited she surprised Em by embracing her to her pillowy bosom and then gave her a huge tip.

Ginger oohed over the photos and said, "The amount of artistic talent in Cottageville is exceptional."

"And Gladys taught many of us," Daniel reminded her.

"That's true. But I was thinking of innate talent, not learned skill. We have so much creativity for a town this size."

"We do," Sarah agreed, putting a forkful of chicken in her mouth. "Thank you so much for feeding me supper." She stood and took her plate to the sink and rinsed it before putting it in the dishwasher. "I'll tackle the dining room while you guys finish your meal. Come on, Whiskey."

The dining room didn't have many places for anything to hide other than a breakfront cabinet that had glass doors on the top half where the crystal and fine china was and two big drawers toward the bottom that housed tablecloths, runners, and cloth napkins plus miscellaneous odds and ends like candles and candle holders and fancy napkin rings.

But Sarah searched it all meticulously in case the necklace was hidden inside of something, though she questioned why anyone would hide it from its original location. That seemed like a stupid and senseless prank.

After that, she moved to the front closet and went through every pocket of every coat and felt inside gloves and mittens and beanies and boots. But Sarah came up empty. The necklace and its velvet box didn't seem to be in the house.

She and Whiskey returned to the kitchen.

"Any luck?" Ginger asked.

Sarah shook her head. "When you are done, can we all look in the garage?"

"But I didn't go into the garage that night," Ginger protested.

"I don't know if it matters. I'm being thorough so that means the garage gets searched too...and maybe even your grounds in daylight hours." Sarah hated what she was about to say next, but she knew it had to be said. "Do you have anything else of value in this house? Anything else that might be missing?"

Daniel and Ginger eyed each other, but Ginger spoke up. "Not really. I mean I have those diamond studs I wear most days and some other semi-precious things."

Daniel added, "And I have the wedding band from before and my wife's engagement ring and wedding band and some of her things. None of it is worth a lot. Oh, and we usually have a little bit of cash on hand."

"Do you have a safe?" Sarah asked.

"We have one ordered. It's scheduled to be delivered tomorrow," Daniel said.

Sarah grimaced.

Very quietly, Daniel added, "And you think that's a few days too late."

"I don't know what to think. But these are the facts as we know them. One, Ginger was gifted an exquisite and expensive necklace that few people knew she had. Two, until mid last week, she had that necklace and it lived in a blue velvet case and she kept it hidden beneath a stack of folded t-shirts in the dresser in your bedroom. Three, last week she showed me that necklace, tried it on for me, and if my memory serves me correctly, she took it off, put it back in its box, and then ran it back upstairs. Four, we held a party last night and eight people came to your house. Five, as of this morning, the necklace and its box are missing. We could speculate that the necklace was stolen in its box. But then that begs the question of when was it stolen? Did you move it from the drawer for any reason after you showed it to me? Has anyone been in your house besides you both, me, and everyone at the party last night?" Sarah looked from Daniel to Ginger and back again.

"I don't think our friends would steal from us," Ginger said.

"Certainly not the group last night," Daniel said.

"Do you think someone else could have been here?"

"But how would they have known about the necklace?" Ginger asked.

"No idea," Sarah said. "But maybe we should call John or Candace and ask them to come dust for prints or something. Just in case."

"We did have some workers here over the last few months," Daniel said. "A plumber, some roofers. An electrician. I mean we did most of the remodel ourselves, but we needed a professional hand or two, plus a lot of delivery people were about."

"But was that before or after you brought the necklace into your house?"

Daniel's eyes rolled to the ceiling like he was thinking.

"Before," Ginger said. "At least most of them. But you are right, Sarah. The necklace and the box clearly aren't here anymore so theft is a possibility. I'll call Candace." Ginger picked up her phone from the kitchen counter.

CHAPTER TWELVE

Twenty-five minutes later Officer Candace Grimes pulled up to the house. Whiskey ran to the front door to welcome her by rubbing against the leg of her uniform. "Hey, Whiskey. How you doing, boy?" She bent and scratched his neck. He looked up at her and grinned.

"Candace, thank you for coming over." Ginger led them into the living room and once they sat, she launched into the story of the heirloom necklace and how it was now somehow missing. Daniel and Sarah remained silent as Ginger told the tale. Candace took notes on a small notebook she had extracted from her jacket pocket.

Ginger ended the monologue with "I'm not sure if it is a police matter—"

But Candace, who had a decade of friendship with Ginger, cut her off. "Necklaces don't possess legs and walk away by themselves. You said you and Sarah searched everywhere."

Sarah interjected at this point. "And I can see her in my mind's eye taking the necklace off in the kitchen after she put it on for me. She secured it back into the box and left me where I sat at the bar to run the necklace back upstairs to put it back where she got it from."

"And did you put it back into the drawer where you said you kept it?" Candace asked Ginger.

"Yes. I wouldn't have put it anywhere else."

"And did you take it out of the drawer after, what was it Wednesday or Thursday?"

"I didn't look at it again after I showed it to Sarah, which was on Wednesday."

Candace eyed Daniel. "And you didn't take it from the drawer?"

"To be honest, I didn't even know where she was keeping it. I watched her receive the necklace from my mother, and we brought it home. But that was the last I saw it, and we had talked about how we would put it in the safe, once that was installed."

"And when will that be?"

"The safe arrives tomorrow. We had to order it and wait for it to come in. The guy who installed our door lock systems also specializes in safes. He's bringing it tomorrow around noon and will cement it into the floor of our walk-in closet under the carpet."

Candace nodded her head. "That's an excellent location. Better than behind framed artwork."

"Have you had any workers in your house since you showed Sarah the necklace, Ginger?"

"No. The only people who have been here were you all last night."

"Do you have security cameras on the front of your house? I didn't notice any as I pulled up."

Daniel answered, "We haven't gotten around to it yet. Plus, well, it's not exactly a high crime area."

Candace said, "That is true, but cameras are great to alert you to when you get a delivery, if wild animals are around, and they can help deter break-ins or even teens looking for somewhere to party. The street you're on, since the houses are far apart and have a lot of land, has been notorious for that for decades."

Ginger and Daniel chuckled, and Ginger said, "I may have been to a kegger near here during high school."

"You're not the only one," Daniel said, brushing his fiancee's hand with his.

"I want to dust for prints in your bedroom. I think we should do the drawer the necklace was in but also the pulls of your other drawers and your nightstand. Was your bedroom door open during last night's party?"

Ginger squinted her eyes like she was thinking, before she said, "We wouldn't have closed it. I didn't know I was coming home to a party." She shot Sarah a questioning look.

"I wasn't upstairs at all yesterday. Jared did take two groups on a tour of the whole house. Candace, you were on the second tour. Was the bedroom door closed?"

"No. All interior doors were open upstairs and down. Okay. So I'll dust the pulls and dresser and front and back door handles. Sarah, I know we have your prints on file. Ginger and Daniel, I'm not sure about yours so I'll take yours when I come back down, so we can exclude you."

"Sounds good," Daniel said.

Ginger said, "I'll go up with you and show you exactly where I kept the necklace."

Whiskey escorted Ginger and Candace up the stairs like he owned the place. Sarah asked Daniel once they were alone, "What do you think? Do you think the necklace could have been stolen?"

"I don't know. It's weird that it was here and now it is not. You've seen our closet and our cupboards. You know Ginger. Everything has its exact place."

Sarah giggled, "Its color-coded place, even."

"At least you knew she organized our closet and it wasn't me." Daniel grinned, displaying straight, very white teeth. "But to think the only people who have been here were you and Jared, Candace, John and Braid, and Em and her guys—all of you are close friends— it doesn't compute that one of you guys would have pilfered it." He narrowed his eyes at the coffee table.

"No, it doesn't."

"And yet you have spent hours deconstructing all of our stuff and spaces and fitting it all back together again and you haven't come across the necklace or the box. So someone taking it seems like the only possibility."

"Could someone have come into your house while you and G

were at work? I mean, most of Cottageville probably knows your hours most days. Even if they aren't conscious of knowing. But I bet if we asked anyone who lives here, they could tell you when to find G at Java and Juice and when you are at Buck and Son."

Daniel nodded his head. "Oh I'm sure they could. And as to someone coming here while we are gone, sure, anything is possible. But no windows have been broken or doors jimmied, and you've seen that the front and back doors both have multiple locks controlled by those keypads and numeric codes."

"Is the code the same for the front and back doors?" Sarah's mind was spinning thinking of all of the ways someone could break into a house.

"Yes. The side door to the garage also has the same locks and system. All have the same code."

"Is there a way to override the code?" Sarah knew the code was Daniel's maternal grandmother's birthdate. Ginger had said they used that as they figured no one would guess it since it was generations removed.

"There's a hidden keyhole so we can use a physical key to open the door." Daniel's mouth opened like he realized something and he stood and started moving toward the kitchen.

Sarah followed him. "How many keys do you have for the doors and where do you keep them?"

"We have five. All of the locks are keyed the same. Ginger has one on her key ring. I have one on mine. We keep a spare in the kitchen drawer. We have another spare hidden in the garage. And then we gave one to my parents, just in case." Daniel opened the drawer in the kitchen that held a flashlight and other miscellaneous but emergency items. He fished around for a second and then held up the key for Sarah to see.

Next they moved to the entryway of the house and from the console table near the door, Daniel picked up a ring with more than a dozen keys. He flipped through it until he found the house key and showed Sarah. "That accounts for two," he said.

Sarah said, "Ginger's purse is sitting on a kitchen bar chair."

They headed back to the kitchen and Daniel rooted in the love of his life's bag until he pulled up an equally full keyring. He fingered the house key and once again showed it to Sarah.

"Garage next?" she asked.

"Might as well," Daniel said. Neither of them put on their coats as they figured they would just be a minute. They crossed the driveway lit only by flood lights attached to the house to the garage's side door, and Daniel typed the code into the keypad. The familiar beeps and sliding of the locks followed. Daniel opened the door and held it for Sarah, who hit the light switch as she entered.

Daniel pulled open the top drawer of the red Craftsman tool chest and showed Sarah the key. "I could call my parents. But I'm sure they have it. So all keys are accounted for."

Sarah frowned for a second. "How many keys are original?"

"Three," Daniel said.

"And where did the other two come from?"

"I made them at the store." Daniel smiled at her.

"Ahh, okay. I just thought if the locksmith guy made them that maybe he made extras you don't know about."

"It's a reasonable train of thought. The lock systems and keys were in sealed packages before he installed them. I didn't have him make keys because, well, I can make all of the keys I want for free."

"Makes sense. But don't you sell locks and door knobs and such?"

"I do, but not as high end as what we have on our doors. I wanted a security expert to create what we have."

"Okay," Sarah said, leading the way from the garage to the house. "So we doubt someone came into your house using a key. Do the keypads record information? Like when someone uses it? Is it wi-fi enabled and connected to an app or anything?"

"Our locks are on the dumber side." Daniel chuckled to himself. "No app. No wi-fi. No record."

"That's too bad," Sarah said, opening the front door of Daniel's house.

Whiskey greeted them, and Sarah could hear that Ginger and Candace were back downstairs. "I hope I didn't smear any potential prints by searching the drawers and removing them and putting them back in," Sarah said.

"Eh. There were a few and some smudges. But we'll see if we have anything when I get back to the station. Daniel, if you'd give me your fingers so I can take your prints, then I'll be on my way."

"Of course," Daniel said.

Ginger asked, "What were you and Sarah doing outside?"

"We were making sure all of the keys for the house are accounted for. While you were upstairs, we were brainstorming ways someone could have come into the house, since we don't think someone from last night walked off with your necklace. And Sarah pointed out, almost everyone in Cottageville knows where we are most days of the week. Someone could have used that knowledge to break into our house while we were at work."

"But then that would mean someone knew I had a necklace to steal." Ginger shook her head. "I told Sarah and Jared and Taylor, but I didn't tell anyone else about it."

Daniel washed his hands after finishing with Candace, who was putting her equipment back into a black nylon messenger bag. He asked quietly, "Honey, when you told them, was it before the cafe had opened for the day or was it when you had customers?"

Ginger frowned, causing wrinkles in her brow.

"I don't remember." She was silent for a couple of beats. Then she said, "Actually, I think Jared brought it up. He said something like Sarah said you got some extra special bling. And I laughed at his description and then told him about the necklace and how it sparkled in the light and how I felt like a princess when I put it around my neck." Her eyes gleamed with unshed tears. "Ugh. I want to feel that way again. Candace, we have to find it."

"Do you have a photo of the necklace? We could send it out to area pawn shops in case it shows up."

"I don't," Ginger said.

"My mom might," Daniel said. "I'm sure there's a photo of my grandmother wearing it somewhere." He pulled out his phone like he was going to call, when Ginger put her hand on his arm.

"Don't call," she said, stress emanating from her like from a bird around a cat. "I don't want your mother to think we are irresponsible."

Candace interjected, "Ginger, we're pretty sure you didn't misplace the necklace. I have to agree that the only thing that makes sense is that it was stolen. Daniel should tell his mother that and get a photo. That's our best chance to get it back."

"But his grandmother had it all that time and it was never stolen. We shouldn't have accepted it until we had the safe." Tears spilled from her eyes.

Daniel wrapped her in a hug. "Ginger, she's not going to be angry. She'll want to help. We aren't responsible for the theft of something we own."

Whiskey pushed himself against Ginger's leg, doing his cattle dog best to comfort her. She looked down at him and gave him a weak smile of thanks.

"You going to be okay?" Daniel asked Ginger.

She sniffed and said, "Probably."

He squeezed her in a hug and kissed the top of her head before releasing her. "I'm going to call my parents. Candace, will you need the actual photo or can we take a photo of it and then text you that?"

"A photo of a photo should be fine. Thanks. And I'll be in touch again as soon as I have some information. Ging, for what it's worth, I think you were right to call. Something doesn't add up. If the necklace isn't here, someone has it. Let's figure that out and make sure you get it back." Then she said goodnight to everyone, and let herself out the front door. They heard the big engine of her patrol car start and her tires crunch a bit of gravel as she drove down the driveway.

"We should probably head out, too. It's getting late and you have an early day tomorrow. I'm sorry we didn't find the necklace tonight, but I'm sure we'll see it again. We'll solve the mystery of what happened to it." Sarah gave her best friend a hug and yelled goodbye to Daniel, who was still on the phone.

"Thank you for being so thorough and for all of your help and emotional support," Ginger said, giving Sarah another hug as they stood at the front door.

"That's what best friends are for. I do think that during daylight hours we should inspect the outside of your house to see if anything doesn't look right or has been disturbed."

"That may have to wait," Ginger said. "I mean, I go to work in the dark. I do come home in the light but that's three to four hours before you are finished."

"Well, maybe you or you and Jared could look around your place tomorrow. Or, will Daniel be here when the safe is being delivered? If so, ask him to do it."

"That's a good idea. Thank you. For everything. Drive safely. And pleasant dreams."

Sarah and Whiskey hopped into the CJ and made their way home. It was almost time for bed.

CHAPTER THIRTEEN

Early Tuesday morning, Sarah was jarred awake by the wail of fire engine sirens. She threw off the covers and ran through her house in her flannel dog bone pajamas and coordinating long sleeve Henley top. Whiskey nipped at her ankles as she went in an attempt to herd her activity.

"Not now, Whisk," she said, throwing open the front door and running in her socked feet down the short driveway onto the street. A police car zoomed past the top of her street headed east. Within a second, an ambulance followed. *What in the world?* Sarah wondered. *Where was the fire? What was on fire?*

She turned toward Mrs. Jenkins' house and scanned the horizon and its shades of grey, infused with soft pinks and peach, for smoke. But she couldn't find any. Just as Sarah turned to go back into her house, she saw across the street, just above the treeline, a flame.

But that made no sense.

Past the woods behind Mrs. Jenkins' house was a flat field that had wildflowers in the late spring and summer, but at this time of year was barren.

And then it hit her. The old water tower. That was the only thing as tall as the trees.

The cold ground seeped into her feet, making Sarah realize she was being stupid. Coming outside in thirty-five degree weather in nothing but her pajamas was the recipe for hypothermia.

"Come on, Whiskey," she said, turning to walk back into the wide open door of her house.

Whiskey followed her and went straight to the kitchen and slurped some water and then hit his food bowl with his paw, like it was time for his breakfast.

Sarah sighed and dumped some kibble in his bowl. While he ate, she changed into insulated running tights, a long sleeve t-shirt and topped it with a sweatshirt, wool socks and her winter boots, and her puffy coat, gloves, and beanie. In a rare occurrence, Sarah grabbed Whiskey's leash, and said, "Let's go." She locked her front door and set off towards the woods.

She jogged at a fast clip with Whiskey running slightly ahead of her on the path that meandered through the trees. The crunch of fall leaves and twigs beneath her boots sounded oddly loud in the otherwise quiet of the morning. As they neared the edge of the wood, the smell of fire grew more pronounced. It wasn't the familiar, comforting scent of burning wood like from a neighbor's fireplace. No. This was acrid, sharp, and chemical. It smelled like kerosene.

Sarah's stomach twisted. The cold of the ground felt like it was seeping through her boots, as if the earth itself was warning her to turn back, to go home where it was safe and warm.

The woods opened up to the large, fallow field. And there ahead of her was the old water tower. It has been abandoned for years, a rusted relic from a bygone era, long out of service, but still standing. Signs posted on it warned people from climbing it.

But what stood in front of Sarah would never be climbed again. Flames engulfed the whole structure, shooting high into the sky. The base was charred and Sarah was sure it would give way and crash to the ground at any minute.

Sarah had stopped and she stared for a moment before calling Whiskey to her side. She hooked the leash onto his collar. "Stay with me, boy." Sarah could see the first responders on the other side of the tower. Hannah Beau and her team, in their thick protective gear, pulled lines of hoses. Sarah frowned and wondered if they couldn't smell the accelerant in the air.

But when one of the firefighters pulled up the hose, even from a distance, Sarah realized that wasn't a normal nozzle. It was huge and shiny metal, and what flew out of it was a thick white foam.

At that moment, the phone in Sarah's pocket rang. She pulled it out and looked at the screen. Chief James.

"Hello, Chief," she answered.

"I see you standing in the field with Whiskey. This is a chemical fire, Sarah. You need to evacuate the area. Leave now. I don't want the Parks to have to take you to the hospital." Wendy and Walter Parks, a married couple, ran the town's volunteer ambulance service.

"Okay, Chief. Thank you for your concern." She disconnected, took one last look at the fire just as the support legs on the water tower gave way and the structure collapsed to the ground.

"Come on, Whiskey. Let's get out of here before that spreads into this field."

Sarah undid his leash to let him run in front of her as they picked up the path and started through the trees. Twenty yards in, a blur of movement to Sarah's right caught her eye. She turned her head and spied someone forging their own path through the trees and brush more than thirty feet away. She could only make out a dark winter coat with the hood up. The person's shoulders seemed wider than hers. But it was hard to tell anything else.

Could this be the fire starter? she wondered.

Without a second thought, she whispered to Whiskey to stop, and then she waited a minute to see where the person was going before deciding to tail them.

Sarah crouched lower, trying to make herself as inconspicuous as possible behind a large, gnarled oak tree. The figure moved quickly and purposefully through the brush, their steps silent but swift. It was hard to tell much about them from this distance, but there was something about the way they moved that set Sarah's pulse racing. The person was surefooted, like they were used to tromping in the woods or on uneven terrain.

Hmm. Sarah told her brain to notice other things about the person. But nothing was coming quickly.

Her breath came out in small, controlled puffs as she turned to look at Whiskey, who was doing his best to stay still beside her, his ears perked.

She glanced back toward the fire but this deep in the woods, it was difficult to see any smoke beyond the trees.

Suddenly Sarah's mind provided her with this thought: the person she was following seemed to know the area. And that meant they were there before the fire was reported. Either before like days, weeks, or months before, and/or earlier this morning. If this person, that she and Whiskey were following started the fire, Sarah wondered if they came at it from her street and woods or from the other side? Did they have a vehicle parked somewhere?

Sarah guessed if so, maybe it was on her side of the woods, otherwise the police would have seen it on the other side.

But why the water tower? Why would anyone burn that?

Her pulse quickened. She admonished herself, *Focus, Sarah. Follow them, find out what they're up to. You can ask questions later.*

Sarah stopped in her tracks as the figure paused for a moment, like they were listening for something. Sarah held her breath. She could hear the crackle of the fire in the distance, but beyond that, the world was eerily still.

After a beat, the person continued on, weaving between the trees. Sarah knew they were north of Mrs. Jenkins' house and even north of Robert Wise's house, which was next to Mrs. Jenkins. The woods eventually stopped at the cross street across from the park. *Did this person park there?*

Sarah's instincts told her that this person wasn't randomly on a stroll through the woods at five a.m. Whoever this was, they were deliberately evading detection. And it wasn't just about the fire—they were heading somewhere. Sarah felt a tight knot in her stomach as the idea that she was witnessing something much bigger than an accidental blaze began to form. This person was up to something, and Sarah couldn't shake the feeling that she might be able to uncover just what it was.

She moved quietly, keeping a good distance, using the thick trees and brush as cover. She had to be careful—if they noticed her, if they knew someone was tailing them, they might bolt...or worse.

Sarah's heart raced as the figure glanced behind them again. Sarah froze so the person wouldn't be attracted to her movement. After a few tense seconds, Sarah took a deep breath and followed, crouching low and keeping her movements slow and deliberate. The woods were denser here, the underbrush thicker. Whiskey was doing well, staying close, but even he had to leap over fallen branches and duck under thick limbs.

They were close now, only a few dozen feet away from the person when it suddenly struck Sarah that there was something about their gait. Something familiar. Sarah's chest tightened. The way the person moved, the way they held themselves—she couldn't put her finger on it, but it reminded her of someone.

The closer she got, the more she felt like a thin wire stretched taut with tension. She had to stay focused. Whatever was going on here—whatever connection this person had to the fire—she needed answers. She was so close to getting them.

In a split second, she lost sight of the person she was following. *Where did they go?* Sarah scanned to her right and scanned to her left but didn't see anyone. *What the heck? They couldn't have just disappeared.*

Sarah crouched down and crept forward, trying not to make a sound. *Surely the person was still here in the woods.* Sarah held her breath, straining for the sound of a twig breaking, of a footstep, or a labored breath.

But then she spied the back of the dark jacket. The person had stopped and was squatting on the ground. They were by a large flat rock, half buried under a blanket of dry leaves. Sarah watched, breathless, as the person lifted the rock slowly and carefully, like they were trying not to create a disturbance or a sound.

What are they doing? Sarah wondered.

Sarah felt a twinge of fear curl in her stomach. *What if they were getting a stashed weapon?*

Her heart skipped a beat when she realized the figure was pulling something from beneath the rock. It looked like a large, black bag—one of those heavy-duty duffel bags. The kind that might carry tools.

A flash of instinct hit Sarah, and she pulled back, retreating a few paces, pulling Whiskey with her. She peered through the thick cover of leaves and branches, trying to get a better view without giving herself away.

The figure pulled something out of their coat pocket and then placed it into the duffle bag, zipped it up, and buried it back under the rock. They glanced around, then made their way toward a nearby cluster of trees, disappearing into the shadows.

Sarah debated if she should follow the person or if she should retrieve the bag. The bag seemed like the safest bet since she realized trying to question anyone could put her in danger, even with Whiskey by her side. She waited for a few heartbeats to ensure the person was actually gone, then slowly and silently made her way toward the spot where the figure had been. She approached cautiously, peering around the large rock. She could feel the weight of the air pressing in on her, thick with uncertainty.

When she reached the spot, Sarah channeled Incredible Hulk energy and pushed against the rock. It was lighter than she expected. She left the duffle exactly where it lay but unzipped it, grateful she was wearing gloves. Her eyes fell immediately on something within, a shiny metal canister, dented and scorched around the edges. A fuel canister.

Sarah's blood ran cold as she realized what she was looking at. The person she'd been following hadn't just started the fire—they'd planned it. And they were still out there.

She grabbed the canister carefully, her mind racing. Whoever this was, they weren't done yet.

Suddenly, there was a rustling sound behind her, and her heart leaped into her throat.

"Whiskey…" she whispered urgently, but before she could pull him close, a voice spoke from the shadows.

"Found something, have you?"

The voice was low, almost amused. And somehow, it made Sarah's skin crawl.

"Don't turn around," the voice ordered as something poked into

Sarah's back. "Or I'll shoot."

Sarah stood as still as a tree in no wind. She held her breath.

A gray sleeve and black glove reached over her and grabbed the duffle bag from her grasp. "Mine," the voice hissed in her ear. "I want you to count to one hundred, aloud so I can hear you. If you turn your head or try to follow me, I will kill both you and Whiskey."

Sarah's eyes went wide. The arsonist knew who she was.

"Start counting. And do it loudly."

"One, two, three..." Sarah's voice rang out as she held fast to Whiskey's collar.

She felt the energy change behind her when she got to ten and realized the person had left. But she still felt she was being watched so she continued, her voice clear. "Eleven, twelve, thirteen, fourteen, fifteen, sixteen..." All the way to one hundred like the person commanded.

Then she turned around and ran as fast as she could through the brush and the trees to her house, her heart pounding in her chest like a marathoner's feet on pavement.

By the time she got to her craftsman bungalow, tears streamed down her face and her whole body shook like a Labrador coming out of the ocean. She shook so violently she couldn't get her key into the lock.

CHAPTER FOURTEEN

"**S**arah," Mrs. Jenkins called to her. "Are you okay?" The almost octogenarian was crossing the street in a long coat and her slippers.

Sarah glanced over her shoulder at her neighbor and before she could say anything, Whiskey trotted to Janice Jenkins and held her fingers in his mouth and led her the rest of the way across the street.

When Mrs. Jenkins was close enough to see Sarah's tear-tracked face, she asked, "What's wrong, dear? Is it the fire?"

Inhaling a shaky breath, Sarah said, "The arsonist held me at gunpoint."

Mrs. Jenkins looked up one side of their street and then the other, as if she were searching for the suspect. "Let's go inside, dear. I'll make you some tea." She took the key from Sarah's hand and inserted it into the lock and opened the door.

Sarah was on autopilot removing her boots and winter apparel, but Mrs. Jenkins stopped her and said, "Sarah, you may be in shock so it would be best if you are going to take those off, to wrap yourself in a blanket or two. Shock can lower your body temperature. Where are your blankets? I'll get you one."

"There's one on the sofa. Thank you."

Whiskey trailed after Mrs. Jenkins. Sarah finished taking off her coat and padded after them, her hands rubbing up and down her arms. Mrs. Jenkins was right. She did feel cold and a bit clammy. She snuggled into the blanket Mrs. Jenkins wrapped around her and pulled her feet up under her on the sofa. Whiskey jumped up onto the sofa and put his upper body across her legs, something he rarely did. She stroked the soft, dense fur along his spine.

"I'm going to make tea, and then I want you to tell me all about what happened." Mrs. Jenkins patted Sarah's shoulder before leaving the room.

As Sarah pet Whiskey with one hand, she gripped her mobile phone with her other. She considered texting Jared, but she didn't know how to begin. *I almost died* seemed too much, though it could have been true. She didn't want to worry him. *I almost caught the arsonist* would lead to too many questions while he was at work. *The water tower is on fire* also seemed to encourage a whole conversation, which she wasn't ready to have. Instead, she kept it simple: "I love you" and pushed send.

Sarah debated calling the Chief, but also figured he'd want to talk to her in person. *I mean, I did disobey his direct order to leave and go home,* she thought. She cringed thinking of how angry he might be once he found that out, how she chose to put her own life in jeopardy by going after the person instead of phoning in a suspicious person alert to the police.

Mrs. Jenkins returned to the living room with two mugs, each embellished with a string and tag. She sat in a chair across from Sarah. "Please start at the beginning," she said, slipping into professional mode. Mrs. Jenkins had spent her career working for various alphabet agencies and government entities around the world. Now, in her retirement, she did some consulting, when and where she was needed.

Sarah explained how the fire engine sirens woke her up and how she had run outside to see where the trucks were going. On her way back in was when she saw the plume of smoke over the trees so she and Whiskey ran through the woods toward where she thought the smoke was coming from, until they got to the field and saw the water tower ablaze, and the firemen and police on the far side of the tower. She explained how Chief James had called her and insisted she go home because the fire was a chemical one. And then how she'd heeded his command, until she saw someone else in the woods and that person, at least from the top half, looked a bit like those grainy photos around town of the tree fire starter. "So I decided to follow them and see where they went," Sarah said, taking a sip of tea. She was finally feeling warmer. "Thank you for the tea. It's warming me from within."

"Good," Mrs. Jenkins said. "And did they catch you following them?"

"Not at first. Whiskey and I did a good job of moving stealthily and being as quiet as possible. We got almost to the end of the woods, I think by the road that runs next to the park. And that's when the person stopped. We stopped too and watched the person move a rock and pull out a black duffle bag and put something in it and then rebury it. Then they left. We watched and waited until I was sure they were gone." Sarah frowned, her brows coming closer together. "Or at least I thought so. Anyway, Whiskey and I went to the rock, and I moved it and opened the duffle bag and found a small, empty container of kerosene. I didn't hear the person approach but they came up behind me and said in a low voice something like 'Found something you like?' I don't remember the exact words. But I do remember the voice gave me a chill. Then next thing I know, something is poked into my back. The person said, 'Don't turn around or I'll shoot' and mentioned me and Whiskey by name. They grabbed the bag from my hands and forced me to count aloud to one hundred. And when I finished and turned around they were gone so I ran as fast as I could back here."

Sarah shivered, recalling it all.

"Can you describe the person you followed?"

Sarah squinted her eyes in thought. "Their coat was gray and their gloves were black. The gray fabric was smooth, like a work coat not a puffer. Do you know those canvas or whatever Carhart jackets that are that mustard color? But it had a hood and the hood was up so you couldn't see hair. The gloves also looked like work or sport gloves, as opposed to leather or knit."

"And when they talked could you tell if it was a male or female's voice?"

"Instinct says male, but the person basically whispered or growled at me so I'm really not sure."

"And when you said boxy, what did you mean?" Mrs. Jenkins' eyes peered over her mug of tea at Sarah.

"Broader shoulders than us. With the jacket on, it hung straight down without a taper. So it looked boxy."

Mrs. Jenkins nodded her head. "So you clearly followed someone you know, or at least who knows who you and Whiskey are. That may make you a target. Especially if the arsonist thinks you can identify them. Did you get those security cameras installed after the last time someone targeted you?"

"We have them but only one has been installed," Sarah admitted.

"With your permission, if you leave them on your kitchen counter, I'll bring Bill over and use my key and we will get those installed in the front and back. And actually, we'll install sensors on your windows and a whole system while you're at work today."

Sarah's mouth was open like a goldfish's. "You don't have to do all of that."

"Nonsense, young lady. We clearly do need to. For the past year you have stumbled upon more mysteries than Sherlock Holmes." She waved her hand. "Okay. I exaggerate. But you know what I mean. And you've put yourself in danger today so I want to ensure you are protected. Get that boyfriend of yours to move back in, too. More people should be a bigger deterrent."

"Unless they just decide to burn my place down," Sarah mumbled.

"Not on my watch," Mrs. Jenkins said with a force that made

Sarah believe her. "How are you feeling right now? Are you over the shock?"

"I think so." Sarah stretched her neck one direction and then the other. She felt tired, like she had finished a 5k run that was mostly uphill. But she had a full day of grooming ahead of her, plus she expected hours of questioning from those she loved, once she copped to this morning's harrowing adventure. "I feel tired, but I am unafraid. Does that make me stupid, after a threat like that?" Sarah looked into Mrs. Jenkins' kind eyes.

"Not at all, Sarah. In my line of work, threats made me angry. As in how dare you try to intimidate me or those I love. But, I was trained to handle that and block out the fear and use the possible peril as impetus for action." Mrs. Jenkins set her empty mug on a coaster on the coffee table. "If you ever want any self defense or weapons training, please let me know."

A shiver ran through Sarah. She hated guns and violence. She didn't want to be in a situation where they were her only recourse.

"It's important to be prepared for anything, if you keep choosing to investigate on your own," Mrs. Jenkins added.

"I understand." Sarah sighed and looked at the time on her phone. She needed to shower and get ready for work. "Thank you for the tea and the talk, Mrs. Jenkins. And for fortifying my home while I'm at work today. I appreciate it and am so glad you are my neighbor." Sarah smiled at the older woman. "And on that note, I still need to shower and get ready for work."

"Of course, dear. Anytime. Just promise me you'll call Chief James today and tell him your story. The police need all of the information possible to do their jobs effectively."

"I will definitely call him. Though I'm sure he'll want to talk to me in person." Sarah stood up and gathered their tea mugs, and she and Whiskey walked Mrs. Jenkins to the door, where they hugged goodbye. Then Sarah double checked all of the door locks in her house before she shut herself in the bathroom to shower.

A half hour later, Sarah scanned every house and yard on her street searching for the gray jacketed person or anything else that looked out of place. She waved to Robert Wise as he passed her on his way to teach music at the high school.

Sarah's eyes darted every which way just like Whiskey checking out the scents since the last time they strolled through the park. A single swing gently rocked in the light breeze. But other than that, the place emitted stillness and peace, with a slight scent of charred pine. When they popped out of the far end of the park, Bill called to them from his front porch. Again, the top of his skull was encased in a trapper hat with the flaps up. A padded and quilted red and black flannel covered his gray sweatshirt. He wore jeans and fleece-lined moccasins on his feet. "Janice called," he said.

"Oh," Sarah said. "If you don't have time—"

He cut her off. "Sarah, I care about you and Whiskey. I am retired and have plenty of time. But most importantly, we—Janice and I and Chief James and Hannah Beau, and everyone else in this town—will do what it takes to keep you safe. I don't need to tell you that what you did this morning was stupid. It could have gotten you killed. You know that. I'm grateful it didn't. And I blame myself for not making sure those security measures were added to your house the last time you had a problem."

Sarah jumped in. "Bill, it wasn't your responsibility. It was mine and I didn't follow through. Just like this morning was stupid. Yes. And you're right. It could have gotten me kidnapped or killed or anything. But the mistake is mine to own. If I died, it would have been my fault."

"Well Whiskey doesn't want to die yet," Bill almost whispered, petting Whiskey between his ears and handing him a biscuit.

Sarah's eyes filled with tears, but they didn't fall down her cheeks. "He doesn't. And I'm not ready either." She leaned down and gave Bill a hug. "Thank you for caring so much about me."

"You make it easy." Bill returned the hug.

"Come on, Whiskey. We need to get coffee and get to work. I'll talk to you later, Bill. Thank you for everything."

Sarah and Whiskey waited for some cars to pass before they crossed Main Street and walked down a block to Java and Juice. The familiar chatter of friends and neighbors welcomed and comforted her as she followed Whiskey like he was the Pied Piper of pastries to the counter.

"Mi'lady," Jared said by way of greeting, as he reached for her to-go tumbler.

"My lord." She held out an imaginary skirt on both sides of her thighs and curtsied.

"Rumor is there's a fire at the water tower." Jared handed her the tumbler back. He had filled it with black dark roast coffee.

Her eyes locked onto his. "Yes. I was there," she said quietly.

"And there's more to that story," he guessed.

She nodded her head once.

"I'll be by after the end of my shift. Double chocolate and cinnamon heart scones? Chicken, pecan, and strawberry spinach salad?"

"Yum. Yes, please. And I look forward to seeing you around three." She paid with her card and then rethought what she just said. "Actually, instead of coming by the Coiffure at three, can you go home to your apartment, pack a bag, and meet me at my house at the end of the day?"

His eyebrows raised as he said, "Yes. But your request feels like *more* than a sleepover."

"You read me clearly, my lord. See you around five-thirty. Have a good day. Come along, Whiskey. We have dogs to groom."

CHAPTER FIFTEEN

For the next two blocks down Main Street and the one block down the street of the Coiffure, Sarah's eyes searched every doorway, intersection, and alleyway for the person with the gray, hooded jacket. She was determined to not get caught again unaware. But no one seemed to be lurking or ready to pounce or fire at her and Whiskey.

She breathed a sigh of relief as she made it to the Coiffure. Sarah unlocked the front door and then relocked it behind her, put the salads in the refrigerator, and sat at a table in the back, sipping her coffee and eating the rich chocolate scone, mentally preparing herself for the day. For the first two appointments of the day, Gladys was bringing her miniature rescue poodles Kahlo and Cassatt for their baths and nail trim before the parade. Sarah looked forward to seeing the woman who was like a second grandmother to her as well as her friend.

But when Sarah heard the front door knob rattle and she peered at Gladys' worried face through the glass, she knew Janice or Bill had been the messenger of the latest news. Sarah opened the door and stepped back to let the dogs and Gladys in, as Gladys rushed her, almost knocking Sarah over in her effort to hug her. "Oh my! I'm so glad you are all right. Gave me a scare, you did," the older woman effused.

"I'm sorry for that. I never want you to worry." Sarah patted Gladys' arm. "Here, let me take their leashes off of them and they can run around with Whiskey." Sarah bent down and unhooked the leashes from Kahlo and Cassatt's tiny pink mesh harnesses. The dogs took off like rabbits at a greyhound track.

Sarah motioned to the sofa in the waiting area. "Do you have a moment? If so, please sit."

Gladys' gnarled fingers fidgeted in her lap as her kind, slightly rheumy eyes bore into Sarah's. "This firebug must be stopped. But you, dear, need to leave that to the professionals. Your sleuthing has been good for our community because you are good at it. But this...this craziness of torching Cottageville landmarks..." Her voice trailed off.

"I know," Sarah quietly agreed. "I know it was stupid and I wasn't thinking. The person is dangerous. But there was something about them. When I was following them through the woods, something kept gnawing at the edge of my mind. Something about the way they moved. I recognized it. But I couldn't piece it together." She surprised herself by what had come out of her mouth. She hadn't even voiced that thought to Janice. Sarah made a mental note to tell Chief James when she talked to him. And then she remembered that she still needed to call him and set up a time to do that. With a very full schedule and only days until the parade, when would she have the time? There was still so much to do.

"So you believe you have seen this person before, that it is someone you know?" Gladys' eyes held Sarah's.

"I think so," Sarah said hesitantly, sounding unsure even to her own ears.

"What was it about the way they moved?" Gladys unbuttoned the top few buttons of her coat, like she was settling in.

Sarah opened her mouth to respond but the front door knob rattled again as Emily unlocked the door and made her way into the Coiffure, a blast of cold air coming in with her. Whiskey, Kahlo, and Cassatt barked and raced to the door to greet her.

"Hey, guys." Emily bent to scratch the ears of all three of her canine friends. When she stood, she said, "Sarah. Gladys. Nice to see you."

Emily walked through the waiting area and opened the hinged counter and stepped through, taking off her coat, gloves, and black beanie to reveal her platinum hair with the red heart accent.

"What fabulous hair," Gladys said. "So artistic."

"Thank you." The grin Emily sported reminded Sarah of a quokka.

"So about the way the person moved," Gladys prodded Sarah once again.

"Yes. It wasn't the walk per se, but how they carried themselves.

Like they were light on their feet, comfortable if you will, moving." Sarah frowned. "I'm not exactly sure what I mean by that."

"It will come to you, love." Gladys patted Sarah's hand. "I'm thankful you are safe. And Janice and Bill and I will make sure you remain so. You can always come to us. Anytime." Gladys used the arm of the sofa to push herself to standing. "I know you have a full day with the parade preparations and all. So I will be on my way."

"Thank you," Sarah said, "for your concern, friendship, and love. I'm so glad you are in my life." Tears welled in her eyes again. She guessed it was just going to be one of those emotional days. She wiped one eye with her fingers and saw Gladys out the door. "We'll see you in a couple of hours," Sarah called after her.

When Sarah turned around, Emily was staring at her, eyes wide, broken-off chunk of scone partway to her mouth. "Why did Gladys say she's glad you are safe? What happened, Sarah? What did you do? And does this have anything to do with the water tower? That's all anyone on the Cottageville social media group is talking about."

"Oh, Em. Let's grab dogs and I'll tell you all about it over their baths." Sarah picked up Kahlo and put her in a tub.

Emily swallowed another bite of scone and drank some coffee, and then she put Cassatt in the tub next to Sarah. Whiskey parked himself between the two tubs to keep an eye on and to provide emotional support to his playmates.

Sarah launched into the story starting with waking up to the sirens and talked nonstop through Mrs. Jenkins helping Sarah into her own home and the plan of adding security. At all of the appropriate spots, Emily exclaimed phrases like "Oh no," and "Are you kidding?", and "OMG," and "Sarah" in a long drawn out sound of exasperation.

When Sarah wrapped up the tale and Kahlo in a towel and walked her to a stainless steel grooming table, Emily said, "You can't get yourself killed, Sarah. I love this job too much."

Sarah chuckled and said, "It's all about you, huh?"

"Well, me and Whiskey," Emily teased. "He doesn't want to live without you either."

"Good to know." Sarah smiled at her assistant. "I love you, too. Both of you."

"More seriously, what did the Chief say? Was he pissed that you didn't go directly home?" Emily rubbed a towel against Cassatt's fur a few times and tucked it under her feet before pulling her from the tub.

"Um, about that. I haven't gotten around to calling him yet."

"WHAT?!" Emily's eyes looked as big as Elmo's.

"I haven't gotten around to it. Janice Jenkins was there when I got home. Then I had to shower and get ready to come here. Then Bill called out to me as Mrs. Jenkins had already called him so I got a mini-sermon from him." Sarah paused as Emily mumbled, "Rightfully so."

"And then I stopped at Java and Juice for our sustenance and... well...java...and then I came here and Gladys appeared soon after I got here. There's the timeline. So sue me that I haven't gotten around to spilling my...um...missteps to the police."

"But isn't that withholding evidence or something? I don't want you to get in trouble, Sarah."

"Oh I may anyway, Em. I mean, I didn't follow Chief James' order. But I also figured he's busy at the crime scene this morning. As soon as I get Kahlo dried and clipped, I plan to call him and ask for a face-to-face meeting. My story isn't exactly something you say over the phone or via text."

"True dat," Em agreed. "Okay. And I'll take the next client or clients if you need to talk to him right away."

"Have you seen the schedule? Both of us will need to bust our butts all day to get through it. Today, tomorrow, and the next two days. This town wants its pets to look good before they step out and parade."

Sarah turned on the fur dryer just as the phone in the pocket of her apron buzzed with an incoming text. She turned the dryer off and set it on the table next to Kahlo so she could pull out her phone.

She exhaled loudly. It was a text from Chief James. "Notice anything or anyone?"

She waited a beat trying to decide how best to respond. *Honesty is always the best policy,* she thought, and then texted "Yep. But a lengthy story is the answer so we need to talk in person."

"You taking a lunch break?"

"A short one," Sarah responded. "Busy week."

"I'll be there at noon."

Sarah relayed that message to Emily as she put her phone back into the apron pocket and started the dryer once again.

Two hours and three and a half dogs groomed later, Chief James opened the green door of the Coiffure. He was in uniform, and it was still mostly pressed and pristine, but tiredness seeped from his gaze and stubble coated his cheeks like he didn't have time to shave this morning. "There's a rumor your house is becoming more secure than Fort Knox," he said by way of greeting. "Do I need to know what that's about?"

"You heard a rumor about my house but not about why?" Sarah asked.

"Something about a threat was made against you. But I'd prefer you to start at the beginning." He plopped himself on the waiting room sofa and pulled a baggie from his pocket. It contained a sandwich of wheat bread, overhanging lettuce, sliced ham, and a pale yellow cheese. He took a bite.

Sarah sat next to him with her salad on her lap and launched into the morning's activities for a third time, but this time, she made sure to include the observations or inklings she had expressed to Gladys.

When she finished, the Chief's sandwich was in his belly and his face wore a scowl. "So your friends are worried this person is going to come after you and Whiskey."

"I think." Sarah stabbed a bite of chicken from her salad and chewed thoughtfully. "But that would be weird, right? Don't arsonists set things on fire because they like to watch them burn? I mean, that's the point, right, if someone is a serial arsonist?" She transferred a strawberry half from her to-go container to her mouth.

"Often. But we aren't sure we are dealing with a serial arsonist."

"How many fires have to happen for the word serial to be attached?" Sarah cocked her head while awaiting the response, just like her dog did on occasion.

"The FBI definition is three or more. When there's two, they call that a spree."

"Semantics," Sarah said. "I think by seeing the person of interest—shall we say—today that we can conclude that person set both the tree fire and the water tower fire. The hooded coat looked like the one in your grainy photos.”

“That’s an assumption. We need facts to tie the two together.”

“The accelerant?” Sarah asked.

“The lab is working on it. But I don’t like that the person pulled a gun on you and threatened your life and knows your and Whiskey’s name. That screams local to me.”

“I know.” Sarah ate more salad though she wasn’t feeling like she had much of an appetite.

“And it explains why Janice and Bill are installing an alarm and sensors, adding extra fire extinguishers, attaching security cameras all over the exterior of your house. If they could figure out a way to repipe it for a sprinkler system, I am sure they would. Sarah, I’ll repeat again what I said when you received that threatening mail and packages last year. Do not walk anywhere by yourself. Do not work here alone. And get Jared or any of your friends to stay with you at your place until we catch this person. I don’t want you taking any more chances. Do you understand?” His eyes felt like lasers searching her soul.

“I do.” Sarah had the urge to make a joke about marriage, but she stifled the snarky comment.

“I will have my people search the woods even more than they have been. From you, we now have a better idea of where to look. But if we can’t find that rock for some reason, when you are done with work today, I may need you to take John into the woods and show him exactly where that duffle bag was hidden. Maybe the person didn’t take everything they hid. Maybe they dropped something. Maybe they made a mistake.”

“We can only hope,” Sarah said. “Of course I’ll help in any way

I can. Just text me and let me know."

"In the meantime, stay safe. Stay alert. And call me immediately if anything else happens or if you remember anything more."

Just as he said that, Sarah remembered one more thing. "That Trident wrapper I gave John from the tree crime scene, was it for cinnamon flavored gum?"

Chief James' eyes sparkled. "Yes, it was." Then he raised his eyebrows in question.

"Whenever the person leaned near my cheek to whisper in my ear, the scent of cinnamon tickled my nose."

Chief James stood and pulled out his phone as he walked to the door. Into the phone he said, "Hey, did we get any prints from that gum wrapper?" He waved over his shoulder to Sarah before leaving the Coiffure and getting into his car which was parked right in front.

CHAPTER SIXTEEN

When five-thirty rolled around and the day was done, Emily insisted on driving Sarah and Whiskey home. "You heard the Chief," she said. "Plus if anything happened, well, I might not forgive myself."

"Ahh, Em. That's so sweet," Sarah said, opening the back door of Emily's Honda so Whiskey could climb inside.

"I'm protecting my paycheck," Emily postured.

"Very funny." But secretly, Sarah appreciated that her assistant wanted her alive and well.

When Emily pulled into Sarah's driveway, Sarah's front door opened. Jared wiped his hands on a dishtowel, while Bill and Janice

Jenkins, who for once out of a tweed suit and wearing a pastel tracksuit in Easter egg purple, flanked his sides. "OMG, Sarah. Bodyguards."

Sarah rolled her eyes. "If you didn't know Mrs. Jenkins was trained and you saw her and Bill, would you be intimidated?" Sarah eyed her gray-haired, wrinkled friends.

Emily laughed in response. "Stay safe, Sarah. And try not to tail any more firestarters."

"Not the plan," Sarah said. "Thanks for the ride home and the excellent work today. I'll see you in the morning."

Whiskey made a pit stop at an azalea bush and then joined Sarah in greeting her friends at the front door. She kissed Jared and hugged Bill and Mrs. Jenkins. "Thank you all for being the welcoming committee. What'd I miss? What do I need to know to function in my own home?"

"Come in and we'll show you," Mrs. Jenkins said.

Sarah usually took another shower after work to rinse away all of the accumulated pet hair and dander, but she understood that would have to wait. She followed her friends into the kitchen, where it smelled of chicken and herbs and rich buttery goodness. Jared had a bottle of white wine open and three glasses poured. He pulled a fourth glass from the cabinet, his eyes questioning Sarah.

"Sure," she said. "It's been a day."

"So I've heard," Jared said, with an underlying meaning of "we will discuss why you didn't tell me yourself later."

Sarah took a sip of wine and then held her glass aloft. "To security and friendship."

They each clinked their wine glass against hers and each

other's before taking a drink.

Whiskey woofed once and hit his empty food bowl.

"I'll feed him," Jared said, opening the freezer to pull out some raw food servings. He microwaved the donut shaped food for a minute before flipping it over and thawing it for another thirty seconds before serving it to Whiskey.

As he did that, Bill asked Sarah to walk with him to her back door and showed her the newly installed keypad and security system. He showed her how to activate it and how to shut it off. He showed her the buttons that with two consecutive pushes summoned the fire department, the police department, or the paramedics. "Don't hit the buttons by mistake. Okay?"

"I'll do my best not to." Sarah took another sip of the light, dry wine.

"The same system is next to your front door, too," Bill said. He opened her back door and motioned with his hand for her to follow him. He pointed to the cameras that were now attached below the roofline to each corner of her house. Those and one five feet up from the door covered the entire backyard. Bill showed her cameras on each side of her house, too, and then three cameras on the front of her house, as well. "These cover your porch, the house itself, the driveway and yard, and they can capture images in the street and across the street to Janice's house. They have a good bit of range," Bill said.

"Wow. You sure that isn't overkill?"

"Not if we are protecting you from being killed, Sarah."

Her eyes darkened at the thought and she frowned.

"Let's go back inside. I'm not sure if the front door is still unlocked, so let's go back the way we came," Bill said.

Whiskey met them at the side yard gate. He must have finished his dinner. He escorted them back into the house.

"Did you show her everything?" Janice asked.

"Cameras, security system..." Bill paused.

"Now for the fire extinguishers," Mrs. Jenkins said. "She opened a cabinet under Sarah's kitchen sink. "You had a very old one in here so we replaced it with a new one that is guaranteed to work."

"Yeah, I think that was a leftover from Gigi."

"We have now tucked one into every room...just in case." Mrs. Jenkins showed Sarah the one in the corner of her dining room, one in the closet by the front door, another in the closet in her guest bedroom, one under each bathroom sink, one tucked into the workbench in her garage, and one in her bedroom closet.

"What about that other bedroom?" Sarah asked. Her house was officially a three bedroom, but the third room with a closet lacked a bed and was mostly used for storage. Boxes with things from her childhood home stood against one wall. A desk and chair were against another. Sarah originally thought the room would make a good office, but she didn't find herself in need of such a space. So instead, the nine by twelve room sat in disarray, rarely visited and unloved.

Mrs. Jenkins said, "I did put an extinguisher in that closet, but It's a small one as I figured odds were you'd never be in there to use it."

"Probably true," Sarah said.

When they went back to the kitchen, Bill asked Sarah to take out her phone and to download an app. All of the cameras around her property could be controlled and monitored via the app. "If it isn't too much of an invasion of your privacy, I'd like Janice and Jared to also connect to your cameras. The more people with eyes on them, the more secure I'll feel about you being here."

Sarah smiled at him and gave him a side hug. "That's sweet, Bill. All three of you can follow my cameras if you want. I have no secrets."

She gave Bill and Janice the wi-fi password for her house. They all downloaded the app and went through the process of scanning a QR code and finding each of the cameras over the wi-fi and connecting those cameras to the app. "

So, you'll be able to see all of these cameras and my house even when you aren't on my wi-fi, right?" Sarah asked.

"Yes, through the app we can see them from anywhere," Bill said.

"Modern technology makes things so much easier than they used to be," Janice said.

"Well, we're almost done here," Bill said.

"Did you talk to the Chief?" Janice asked Sarah.

"I did. We ate lunch together. He had already heard you were fortifying my house so he came into the Coiffure and asked why. That's how he started the conversation. But I had already messaged him to set up the meeting."

"Good," Mrs. Jenkins said. "It looks like the crime scene techs have been combing the woods and field all day."

"Oh that's right," Sarah said, "the Chief said I may need to show John Beams where the duffle bag was. I should text him." Sarah picked up her phone from the counter and asked Officer Beams if they needed any help.

"Would you like to stay for supper?" Jared asked Bill and Mrs. Jenkins. "I made plenty."

"That's mighty kind of you," Bill said. "I'd love to. Come on, Janice. What do you say?"

"Yes," Mrs. Jenkins said. "Thank you."

Sarah grabbed four sets of silverware, four placemats, and four cloth napkins. "Are you plating in here?" she asked Jared.

"Yes," he said, pulling four dinner plates from the cupboard.

Sarah set the dining table and added four glasses with water plus the rest of the wine bottle on the table. Her phone chimed with an incoming text. It was John Beams saying he thought they found the place. A second chime signaled a photo. A third chime indicated words to accompany the photo: *Is this it?*

The photo showed a semi-flat rock with the area of leaves and debris around it disturbed. It looked similar to the rock that covered the duffle bag. But where was this rock in the photo? That's the question she texted to John.

He responded, "Maybe ten yards from the street and thirty-five yards from the park parking lot. It was the only area that looked like something that was not disturbed by footfalls or walking. This looked dug up."

"Okay. Sounds about the right spot. I can come to it, if you need me."

"You've been through a lot today. Maybe tomorrow. Have a good night."

Sarah smiled at the text, appreciating all of her friends and loved ones looking out for her and her well-being. She sighed as Jared, Bill, and Janice entered the dining room with full plates of food. Jared carried hers and set it at the head of the table. Chicken piccata; wild rice pilaf; and vibrant steamed carrots, green beans, and red pepper slices enticed her from their artful arrangement on the plate. *How did she get so lucky to find a love who loved to cook and did so beautifully?* She gazed at Jared with affection in her eyes. And even though this morning her life had been threatened, tonight she felt nothing but love from those in her home and in her town, though she knew that Jared would have a million questions for her once their guests left for the night.

And she wasn't wrong. They spent the dinner hour talking about the pet parade and Janice's last contract job in Spain—at least what she could safely divulge—and the volunteer work Bill was doing at the elementary school helping kids with their reading and basic math. Jared told them about his upcoming book release and the tour his publisher was planning, and he showed them photos on his phone from the next book in his graphic novel series, a manuscript his publisher expected to receive from him in the fall.

Bill and Janice appropriately oohed and ahhed over Jared's drawings and they asked him questions about other mediums of art he liked.

When they seemed to run out of topics, Sarah mentioned the search she did at Ginger's the night before for the missing necklace, and that launched a litany of questions from Bill and Janice, who was somewhat of an authority on heirloom jewelry.

"But there isn't a photo of the necklace?" Janice asked.

"Daniel thinks someone in his family has one. But no, Daniel and Ginger didn't take one."

"That's too bad," Janice said. "Recent photos make it easier for law enforcement and for insurance companies and claims."

Sarah's forehead creased. "They didn't say anything about making a claim. Ginger wasn't quite convinced it was stolen, though I don't see how it couldn't have been."

"You said they have numbered locks but that they have a key override function?" Bill asked.

"Yes." Sarah took a sip of wine.

"And who installed them?" Bill asked.

"A security company," Sarah speared a green bean. Its color reminded her of Jared's eyes.

"Licensed, bonded, and insured?" Bill asked.

"Most likely. Daniel wouldn't have done it any other way, I don't think."

"Local company?" Janice asked.

"I believe so."

"And nothing else was taken?" Jared asked.

"They didn't think so."

"Who knew she had the necklace?" Janice intertwined her fingers over her plate, which made Sarah think she was in investigative mode.

"Daniel. Ginger. Daniel's parents. Me as of last week. Ginger said she talked about the necklace to Jared and her other employee Taylor but she couldn't remember if the cafe was open or if it was before business hours. I asked."

"So a very small group of people," Mrs. Jenkins said. "And do we know who has been in her house?"

Sarah rattled off the list of names of people from Sunday's party.

Mrs. Jenkins' expression was neutral, almost unreadable. But she said, "In my experience, losing one item to theft, one very specific item, but nothing else, usually means the thief was looking for that particular item."

"But the only people who knew and were also in her house were me, Sarah, and Taylor," Jared said, "and none of us would have taken the necklace."

"That may be true," Mrs. Jenkins said. "That is who was in the house that you know about and who knew about the necklace. But the question remains, we don't know who entered the house without anyone knowing or who anyone told about the necklace, even casually."

"I didn't tell anyone except Sarah and I talked about it after she saw it," Jared said, putting his hand atop Sarah's.

"We don't know if Taylor told anyone," Sarah said. "Or if Ginger was overheard telling you guys about it."

"And the way this town loves to talk, really anyone could have known about it," Bill said. "Or Daniel's mom could have told the ladies in the gardening club or the Rotary or the quilting group or anyone that she gifted the necklace to Ginger. We just don't know."

Sarah shook her head. "This mystery is more complicated than I thought."

"The good ones always are." Mrs. Jenkins said. "But those are the most satisfying to solve. So the police have checked for prints?"

"Yes."

"Maybe it will be in the system and easy to piece together," Bill said.

But Sarah had a feeling that wasn't going to be the case.

CHAPTER SEVENTEEN

After they said goodnight to Janice and Bill, took Whiskey into the backyard to do his potty last call, and secured all of the locks on Sarah's house, Sarah and Jared went into the kitchen to finish the dishes. Whiskey didn't follow them. He was stretched out on the living room sofa, paws sporadically moving as if he was chasing squirrels in his sleep. Sarah loaded the dinner plates into the dishwasher and said, "Thank you so much for making us supper. It was delicious."

Jared wrapped his arms around her from behind and kissed the top of her head. "You're welcome, Sarah." His voice sounded rough like he was fighting strong emotion. "I'm not gonna lie. Hearing what happened to you today crushed something inside me. I couldn't stand it if anything happened to you. And I felt let down that you didn't tell me about it yourself."

"I wanted to tell you," Sarah protested, "but I didn't know how or when. I couldn't tell you at the cafe with all of those people there and you working. And it wasn't exactly something I could text." She strained her neck to look up into his eyes and was surprised to find him on the verge of tears. That made her own eyes well and her heart feel like it was twisting in her chest. She never wanted to hurt him. "I'm sorry," she whispered. "I am so, so sorry." She placed her hand against his cheek.

He hugged her tighter and bent his head so that his lips met hers. The kiss was sweet and tender and triggered the tears to spill from Sarah's eyes. The tears were full of so much: regret, relief, love, and the unspoken fears she'd been carrying all day. They ran down her cheeks as if washing away the weight of everything unsaid, leaving her bare and vulnerable in his arms.

"Let's finish cleaning up and get ready for bed. You have an early day tomorrow, and since Chief James doesn't want me walking to work by myself, Whiskey and I will go in when you do."

Sarah broke their embrace to return her attention to the dishwasher.

"But that's hours before you open," Jared said. "Why don't you stay home and then have Mrs. Jenkins walk with you, or you and Whiskey could drive to the Coiffure?"

Sarah was surprised she didn't think of that second option. It was a reminder to her of how ingrained habits were. She had walked to work almost every day for the past seven years; it never occurred to her to do anything else. She cherished that time, the quietness and solitude in the early mornings when few others in Cottageville were out and about, the tranquility of the park's wide open spaces and all of the amazing memories that had been created on its grounds, including last year's award that she won, being named Cottageville's Citizen of the Year.

Sarah wondered if that's how the firestarter knew who she and Whiskey were. Most of the town came out for December's Winter Wonderland, when Mayor Trish gave her the award and posed for photos with Sarah—and those photos and the related article were published in The Cottageville Courier—and lit the big pine (that was now the fire casualty) to kick off the holiday season. Or, was the arsonist someone she actually knew, a friend, a neighbor, an acquaintance, or a client? Sarah scowled. Unease gripped her gut thinking the fire starter could be someone she knew and maybe even knew well. Or at least someone she thought she knew well.

"Hey Sarah, where'd you go?" Jared's hand waved in front of her face.

"Sorry," she said. "I was ruminating on the fact that the person who held a gun on me knew my and Whiskey's names. I don't like the idea that they could be someone I know and maybe know well."

"We don't know that. You do realize that you're a bit of a celebrity around here, right? You've been in the paper, you got the award from the mayor, you helped solve five crimes. People talk about you on the local social media. I know you don't follow it, but every time something big happens in this town, it's gotten so that someone writes in the responses 'wonder how long it will take Sarah to solve it.' Some guy even wanted to start a betting pool that you'd figure out who lit the tree on fire before the police did."

"What? That's crazy. The police have all that training—"

"And yet you've helped them close cases." Jared caressed her back.

Sarah leaned against his caress, and then she turned to face him. "You do know that I am not in competition with Chief James and his team, right?" Her eyes searched his for understanding.

"Of course I know that. But I also know you have a gift, a knack for figuring out mysteries. And it would be a shame to not use that gift."

"Even when it puts me in harm's way?"

"Mi'lady, while I don't like when you're in harm's way, as you put it, I acknowledge that anyone who wants to be with you would do you and themselves a disservice to try and squash your natural curiosity, inquisitiveness, and ability to piece together puzzles, even when others can't quite understand how everything fits together. I'm grateful you have allowed me along for the ride." He kissed her again, a little deeper this time.

When they broke apart, Sarah said, "I think you forgot luck. Sometimes I'm just lucky, like when I stumbled on what was going on at the pop-up candy store. That was totally luck, not skill."

"True," Jared agreed. "But you're still my super woman." He intertwined his fingers with hers and pulled her out of the kitchen, turning lights off as they went.

The next morning's alarm went off too early for Sarah. She squinted at Jared as he climbed out of bed in the dark and headed into the bathroom to shower. He was due at Java and Juice at four-thirty. Whiskey repositioned himself in a ball against Sarah, soaking up some of her warmth. He sighed and started to snore within minutes.

Sarah herself wasn't so fortunate. She lay awake listening to the water cascading in the shower, the sound of Jared humming, the water stopping. He emerged from the bathroom fully dressed and Sarah asked, "How'd you sleep?"

"Okay. But shouldn't you be asleep?" He bent over her and pressed his lips against her forehead.

"Your alarm woke me and my mind is too busy to go back to sleep."

"Need to talk about anything?" He rubbed her shoulder.

"Nah. Just going through the lists of what needs to be done still for Saturday. Puzzling over the situation with Ginger's necklace. You know, life stuff." Sarah smiled in the darkness.

"Makes sense," Jared said. "I'm always here for you, mi'lady."

"I know." Sarah grinned. "And that makes me so happy. I love you, Jared." She disturbed her cattle dog who let out an audible exhale when she reached toward Jared and clung to him in a hug.

He ran his hands over her back. "I love you, too. And if I don't let you go right now, I'll find ways to make myself late for work."

Sarah giggled. "Okay, lover. I'll see you in a few hours."

"Sounds good. And please, either drive, or bring an escort. Don't walk anywhere by yourself...or with just you two. I know Whiskey would do everything in his power to protect you, but he is ineffectual against a bullet shot from a distance."

"I promise," Sarah said. "Now get going. I don't want Ginger to blame me if you are late."

"And she totally would." Jared's laughter filled the bedroom.

"Oh I know. Sorry dog, but I need to get out of bed and use the bathroom."

Whiskey sighed again and stretched into the space she vacated.

Jared called after her, "I'm turning off the alarm before I open the door. Please reactivate it before you shower." Bill had stressed that they added no interior motion sensors because they didn't want Whiskey to accidentally set off the alarm if he got up during the night and moved about the house. The alarm literally monitored all of the doors and windows, the exterior and perimeter of the craftsman bungalow.

"Will do," Sarah said, shutting the bathroom door. While she was in there, she decided to get into the shower while the water was still warm...and forgot all about reactivating the alarm.

Thirty minutes later, Whiskey had been in the backyard to do his business, had eaten his breakfast, and was now back in bed, and Sarah sat at the dining room table, looking at the Valentine's Day parade to-do list spreadsheet at what wasn't marked as done. Her hands were wrapped around a mug with Whiskey's face on one side of it, absorbing the warmth from her first coffee of the day.

The swag for the costume competition winners was the only thing on the list that hadn't been checked off. Sarah grabbed a legal pad and a pen and walked her coffee mug from the dining room to her multi-purpose storage room, otherwise known in real estate descriptions as that third bedroom. She turned on the light and knelt next to the first box in the room, which was marked in Sharpie: V-D-P DONATIONS. Sarah opened the box flaps and peered inside. She pulled out all of the contents and spread it on the floor around her. The big box pet store in the next town over had donated four plush and squeaky dog toys: a hedgehog, an alligator, a brown mixed breed puppy, and an orange and white striped cat. Sarah figured a canine recipient of the cat might try to tear it limb from limb. Though any of the toys were bound to be dissected of their squeakers and stuffing. It was what many dogs did.

Ginger had donated six gift certificates to Java and Juice for the judging. And six other restaurants and bars in town—the full-breakfast hotspot Poached Perfection, the Indian fast-food take-out Quick Curry, Luigi's Pizzeria, Butch's Brewery, Chuck's Grill, and Donna's Donuts—had donated either gift cards or t-shirts emblazoned with the establishment's name and logo, or both. Carole Binds had donated three brand-new hardbound books on behalf of the Cottageville library, whose side facing Main Street had been rebuilt after a big rig had lost control and crashed into the plate glass and steel side of the structure, causing much damage at the end of the previous year. Carole said she wanted to remind Cottageville residents that all of the programs had recently resumed.

Buck and Son had originally thought to donate products for pets to the parade, but then Daniel thought otherwise, expanding on the idea so that all pet participants were to be gifted with a ten dollar gift card to the hardware and more store. Sarah was stunned at his generosity, as that meant he had donated two hundred ten dollar gift cards, a sizable chunk of change, if they were all used.

Sergio had donated full-size bottles of his favorite shampoo for humans to be included in the prize winners' bags, as well as discount coupons for fifteen percent off any service at his salon. And of course, Sarah herself had donated free nail clipping service for each of the prize bags.

The things that were missing were the t-shirts she had ordered for the humans of the pets whose costumes would win. She had ordered six large red t-shirts. On the front of each shirt was "My pet won at the Valentine's Pet Parade" and one back was the town crest and "Cottageville, established in 1850," and the red and white bandanas. She scrolled through her email to find the ship confirmation and clicked "tracking". The package said it was due at the Coiffure late this morning. Sarah exhaled the anxiety she was holding that the final prizes wouldn't make it in time.

Everything seemed set. The parade and festivities should go off without a hitch...as long as nothing else in town was set on fire, like at the park, on Main Street, or anywhere else along the route. Sarah said a quick prayer that she and Whiskey and the participants and everyone else in their town would be kept safe and that the police would quickly catch the person responsible, the person who favored a gray jacket and sugar-free cinnamon chewing gum. Sarah shivered at the memory of how close she came to not being alive to run the parade.

"Stop it," she commanded herself. "It's not productive to go there." And just like that she remembered that she didn't re-engage her house alarm.

She flipped off the lights in the spare room and padded through her house, looking out windows into the darkness, wondering if she were being watched, wondering if the arsonist was making more plans to set more things ablaze...or to ensure that she could never reveal their identity.

Not that she could.

As much as she had thought about it and turned every clue over in her mind, she couldn't figure out what had triggered a familiarity. She knew her subconscious was churning through her memories, trying to bring something to consciousness, but that thing eluded her like a squirrel hidden in a treetop did to Whiskey. He knew it was there and that it was calling to him, but for the life of him he couldn't pinpoint its location let alone catch it in his powerful jaws to consume.

Sarah stopped by the backdoor and typed the code into the keypad that caused a beep and turned on a green light, signaling the alarm was engaged. She went into her kitchen and quartered an apple and ate it with some peanut butter, while standing at the kitchen counter. She wasn't used to being up so early and being so idle. In fifteen minutes, she and Whiskey would normally leave for their walk, but they would have to skip that today. Sarah frowned. She liked the exercise and the fresh air.

Maybe Jared was right and she should ask Janice Jenkins to accompany her. The older woman was usually an early riser. Sarah walked to the front of her house and looked out an entryway window. Two lights were on inside the first floor of Mrs. Jenkins' house, as well as her porch light.

Sarah pulled her phone from the pouch of her goldenrod Mount

Barkmore hoodie and texted her neighbor. "Would you be up for a walk?"

Mrs. Jenkins' response was prompt and efficient. "Let's go."

"Whiskey," Sarah called. "Want to go for a walk?"

The dog ran so fast from the bedroom that he slid on the hardwoods and stopped against the front door. He popped to all four feet and grinned at her like that was the most fun he had had in his life.

"You crack me up," Sarah said, putting her arms into her puffy coat and then zipping it and putting a blue beanie over her hair. Sarah pocketed her house keys and some poop bags, and she opened the front door, which caused the alarm to beep two times in succession. She pulled the door quickly shut, not wanting to trigger the alarm siren.

Mrs. Jenkins was exiting her own house just as Whiskey and Sarah reached her front steps. She wore a long deep chocolate covered wool coat, an off-white nubby scarf, and matching knit hat with a pom pom on top. "Good morning," Sarah called. "Thank you for walking with us."

"Of course, Sarah," Mrs. Jenkins said. "I meant what I said about being here for you. I know your schedule and have planned accordingly."

"Thank you. Jared suggested I could skip the walk and drive to work."

"Walking your dog is important to both of you. I'm happy to accompany, though I don't move as fast as I once did."

They walked up the hill and through the empty park and straight to Bill's house, where they found him as always, bundled up against the cold but sitting on his front porch with a cup of coffee and the local newspaper. The paper was in his hands, the double-page spread open. His eyes peered over the top at them. "Morning, ladies."

A large image above the fold of the paper caught Sarah's attention, and suddenly her mind lit like a struck match, blazing with recognition. The headline above the image declared: *Star Quarterback Chooses OSU.* The photo was of Caleb Bupp, in his CHS uniform, his arm stretched in a pass, football whizzing through the air to someone out of the range of the camera. Sarah had watched him play weekend after weekend over the past four football seasons. Since Cottageville lacked a college, high school sports were a big deal, with most of the town coming out to sit in the stands and cheer on the local teens.

And Caleb Bupp possessed talent like few Cottageville high school athletes had in decades. He had been courted by the top football schools in the country: Ohio State, the University of Michigan, Penn State, Bama, Texas A&M, the University of Texas, the University of Florida, the University of Georgia, and LSU. Sarah had heard rumors that agents and scouts and his father had been pressuring Caleb to sign lucrative NIL deals, to secure his future, and because his parents' farm had been failing.

Sarah's mind's eye ran a short film of the way the arsonist walked through the woods and compared it to the way the quarterback walked onto the field, and she was almost sure they were one in the same. A lump formed in her throat and tears pooled in her eyes. *Why would Caleb do something that would destroy his life?*

CHAPTER EIGHTEEN

The rational part of Sarah's mind tried to argue with what she perceived as truth. No one deserved to be convicted—even in one's thoughts—without a trial and a jury of their peers. But she felt certain that the person she had followed was Caleb Bupp, and that's why the way he moved looked familiar. She had seen him on the field, working his light-footed magic. She had seen him and his buddies tromping around town, hanging out, running in the park, and enjoying life. She had recognized the way he moved. And she knew how the town considered him a kind of hero, a golden boy with a golden arm.

And that recognition now made her sick to her stomach.

"Sarah, are you okay?" Bill asked, jarring her from her thoughts. "You are pale like you've seen a ghost. Why don't you sit down? Janice, can you go into my house and get Sarah a glass of water. Pour some coffee for yourself, if you want."

Sarah sat in a wooden chair next to Bill, who folded his newspaper into half and then half again, gathering it in front of him. Sarah debated relaying her suspicions to Bill, but sensed that the first person she should talk to was the Chief. She didn't want to be a rumor-starter without evidence or cause—or even with it for that matter; Cottageville possessed enough loose-lipped people as it was.

"I'm okay," Sarah said. "But I just thought of something I need to tell Chief James. Is it okay if I go into your house and make the call?"

"Of course, Sarah," Bill said. "I'll keep Whiskey with me right here. Want another treat, boy?"

Whiskey was content to sit against Bill's shins and get scratches and treats all morning, if that was on offer.

Sarah opened the door to Bill's as Janice was coming out so she relieved Janice of the glass of water and held the door for her as she passed by onto the porch. "I'll be back out in a minute," Sarah said.

She walked into Bill's kitchen, which was the furthest room from the front porch, and took a sip of water before she pulled up Chief James' contact information and pushed "call."

The Chief answered on the first ring. "Good morning, Sarah."

Sarah took a deep breath and then said, "I remembered something about the arsonist." Then she explained how something kept nagging at her about the way the person moved, like it was familiar, but that she couldn't tie it to a person until she saw Bill's newspaper. "I know this is speculation as opposed to evidence, but I have seen Caleb out and about with those loose fitting jeans and he does have a distinctive walk."

"I wonder if he's a fan of cinnamon gum," Chief James said. "We found another wrapper near the water tower."

"Oh my gosh!"

"Thank you for calling with your suspicions, Sarah. It was the right thing to do."

"I debated, you know. I felt bad for making an accusation, but..." Words failed her.

"We'll bring him in for questioning. Please keep your thoughts to yourself for now."

"Of course, Chief." They disconnected, and Sarah drank half the glass of water before going back out onto the porch. Whiskey was still sitting against Bill like he had found a new BFF.

"I appreciate the water, Bill, and the use of your home. Janice, I'm afraid I need to get back home, grab the CJ, and get to work. For now I've been sworn to secrecy about what Chief James and I talked about. I'm sure you understand." Sarah leaned down to give Bill a side hug as Janice rose from her chair.

"I'll make sure she gets home safely," Janice said to Bill. "And then I'll return here and cook you breakfast. I figure Gladys will be by soon. Maybe she and those poodles can join us."

"Sounds good. Thank you." Bill unfolded his paper and opened it and continued reading.

As they walked back through the park with Whiskey leading the way, Mrs. Jenkins said to Sarah, "You realized something instrumental, didn't you? But you didn't like where those dots you connected led."

"How did you know?" Sarah turned her head to the left to get a look at Janice, who was walking by her side.

"Too many years of experience, too much life lived. Sometimes the most difficult situation in sleuthing and uncovering truths is that we may not be emotionally prepared for the answers. Or we may feel too much empathy about why a person or people did a particular thing. It's like when a woman fights back against a rapist and kills him. We may subscribe to the concept that murder is wrong, but not want to follow the letter of the law regarding her actions. Or like how I sought vengeance after my husband's death." Mrs. Jenkins nodded her head like she was agreeing with her own words. While much of Mrs. Jenkins's history had a long-buried secret, eventually parts of the story seeped into the town and were now embedded in its lore deeper than the Mariana Trench.

Quietly Sarah said, "I wish the person I suspect is the arsonist was someone else, someone without so much to lose, or someone not so nice."

Mrs. Jenkins smiled knowingly. "Have you ever watched any of those true crime documentaries about serial killers?"

"Umm, yes, maybe a few," Sarah joked since Em kept her up to date on true crime podcasts and they had occasionally rehashed documentaries on Ted Bundy, Jeffrey Dahmer, and John Wayne Gacy, who was known as the Killer Clown.

"Know what the most common thing that is said by their neighbors and their colleagues?" Janice asked as they reached the top of their street.

They waited for a car to pass before crossing. Sarah remained silent, figuring Mrs. Jenkins would answer her own question.

"That they are nice. Their friends, neighbors, and colleagues almost always talk about how nice they are. While the arsonist may not be a killer, they are a person who could be having a mental health crisis or feel like their life is out of control—and starting a fire is something they can control—or they could be doing it as a way to get attention."

Sarah pursed her lips. *Caleb Bupp sure has gotten a lot of attention,* she thought. But she could see him feeling out of control with all of the pressure. *He threatened to kill you and Whiskey,* she reminded herself, trying not to fall into the trap of feeling too bad for him, if he was indeed the fire starter.

"Thank you for all of the support, the walk, and the psych profile inside the mind of someone committing crimes." Sarah grinned at Mrs. Jenkins.

"Of course, dear. And I hope that when you can confide in someone, you can tell me what you remembered. Shouldering a burden alone makes for a twice as heavy load as when the weight is split between two people." She offered Sarah a stiff hug, before she climbed the stairs to her house. Then she turned and watched as Sarah made her way across the street and inside her house.

Sarah turned off the alarm as soon as she entered the front door. Then she ran into the closest bathroom and peed, grabbed her to-go tumbler from the kitchen and then her purse and car keys from a table by her entryway. She turned on the alarm and then she and Whiskey went back out the door.

In five minutes, they parked in front of Java and Juice and Whiskey jumped over Sarah to get out the door like there was no way she was going inside without him. He was determined to get one of Ginger's special chicken dog treats.

The cafe was half-full, with Mayor Trish, in a wool suit with a skirt and knee high boots, and Barbara, attired in a purple fitted tank top and purple yoga tights, sitting at the table closest to the door. "Hey, Whiskey. Morning, Sarah," Mayor Trish called out. "Are you ready for Saturday?"

"We are. The last couple of prizes arrive this morning. Everything else is done."

"My office has received a lot of calls from people concerned about replacing the tree."

"That's great. Have you been telling people about your booth?"

"We sure have. I can't wait for Saturday to get here."

"It's going to be so fun," Barbara said, biting into a chocolate and cinnamon heart scone. "Mmm mmm. These are so good. I'll need to take two classes today to burn off the calories."

Trish chuckled. "Babs, you know you look fabulous all of the time."

Whiskey had wandered across the cafe to the counter and was waiting patiently in the short line. He sat on his haunches with his eyes straight ahead, focused on Jared. Sarah joined him and patted his head. "Thanks for saving a place in line for us, Whisk."

When their turn at the counter occurred, Sarah handed her tumbler to Jared, who asked, "Did you walk this morning?" He reached over the counter to slap Whiskey five and to hand him a biscuit.

"Yes, with Janice. And we drove here."

"Good. Same scones? I made you and Em special salads and they are on me."

"You didn't have to do that." Sarah beamed at him.

"But I did." Jared handed her a bag, and she handed him cash for her coffee.

"You're the best boyfriend ever." She leaned across the counter and smacked his lips with hers.

At that moment, with her blonde hair in a high ponytail and a Java and Juice apron covering her clothes almost all of the way down to her Chuck Taylors, Ginger came out of the back room and said, "I'm not paying you to kiss the customers."

"Very funny," Sarah said. "Hey, Ging, did you ever figure out when you told Jared and Taylor about the necklace?"

"It was early morning and we were in the kitchen prepping the pastries," Jared said. "I remembered at some point during the night and woke up with the answer."

Ginger's eyes looked like a dimmer switch had been increased to fully on. "That's right. I was mixing the scone batter and you and T were chopping stuff for salads. The blueberries reminded me of the sapphires and that's when I opened my mouth."

"And did you learn if Daniel's parents told anyone?"

"Only people in the family, his mother said."

"I'm determined to figure it out," Sarah said.

"I'm sure you will," Ginger said. "We count on you for that."

"Okay, gotta go. Dogs to groom. Nails to clip. Glands to express."

"Ick," Ginger replied. "Better you than me."

Sarah and Jared chuckled. "Come on, dog. The Coiffure awaits."

Sarah and Whiskey hopped back into the CJ and drove the few blocks to their business. Emily was already inside with the lights on. She sat at the back table, her face hovered over a textbook. A tumbler of coffee sat next to the book.

"You're early today," Sarah said by way of greeting.

"Big test tonight," Em said, before looking up. "Hey, Cottageville social is going nuts this morning. Caleb Bupp got pulled over on his way to school. So many people are speculating."

Tightness gripped Sarah's heart space. "What are they saying?" She put the scones on the table next to Em and her own coffee next to the bag. She pulled out the salads and noticed that every strawberry and carrot and cucumber and piece of chicken had been cut into hearts in both salads. "Holy cow. Check this out." Sarah shoved a salad under Emily's nose. "Jared said he made them special for us and he paid for them. Aww, how sweet is that."

"Sickeningly." Em grinned. "But stuff like that might make him a keeper. Anywho, the speculation on Caleb ranges from busted with performance-enhancing drugs to expired tags to breaking into his coach's house...because apparently someone did. But whoever broke into the coach's house supposedly only took one thing, a signed football. Nothing else."

"Who signed the football? Was it valuable?"

"Some football players from the Steelers in the seventies, I think. I dunno."

"Sounds like it could be worth something. The Steelers won a bunch of Super Bowls back in the day."

Emily shrugged as if she didn't care.

"Hey, do you know if anyone else mentioned missing an item of value at their house?"

"Not that I know of, but we could probably search the social using a keyword like 'stolen' or 'missing' or 'break-in' and see what pops up."

"When you have time, like maybe over lunch, could you do that for me? If only one item was stolen from the coach's house while jewelry and other things of value were left, it sounds like what happened at Ginger and Daniel's."

Emily took a sip of her coffee. "And I'm sure having only one thing go missing makes you think you misplaced it. That could make you overlook a theft or make you think you're going crazy. As in 'I thought I had it right here.' That's a cruel way to mess with people."

Sarah hadn't thought of it like that. But Emily was right.

CHAPTER NINETEEN

At eleven the last box of prizes for the parade arrived at the Coiffure and Em squealed over the cuteness of the shirts and bandanas. "Can I have a bandana, Sarah, please?"

"If there's enough. I forget how many I ordered."

Emily counted aloud and when she was finished, Sarah, who was trimming the fur on a terrier, told her, "Yes, go ahead and take one. But I expect you to have it on your person somewhere while you help at the parade."

"Absolutely," Em said, drawing out the ab on the word.

At noon, Chief James stepped into the Coiffure, this time without a sandwich, but he was more jittery than usual, like he had been connected to a coffee IV for the past eight hours. The shadows under his eyes had puffed into bags and his hair stuck out from his head underneath his service cap. "Sarah, do you have a moment?"

Two minutes before, Sarah had sat at the table with her salad in front of her and a glass of water by her side. She had exactly twelve minutes until their next client was due and she was determined to take a breather and inhale her food.

"Want some salad?" she offered.

"No, you eat. I'll talk. But can we head somewhere more private?"

Emily was blow drying a border collie, but she must have heard over the hum of the dryer because she said, "Don't mind me. I'll put my headphones on." She dug black Beats over- the-ear headphones from her backpack, connected them to her phone, and turned on some tunes.

Sarah nodded her head toward the back room anyway, and Chief James followed her. She ate while he talked.

"We talked to Caleb and he copped to starting the fires." The Chief audibly exhaled and Sarah felt the pain radiating from him, of disappointment, of the knowledge of devastating the town, of hopes dashed and dreams ruined.

Even though her mouth was full of salad, Sarah eked out a "Why?"

"Stress. He felt like he had no say or control over anything in his life. Pressure at home to be a good student, be the best athlete, be perfect. He cracked. Or was cracking. He sobbed as he told us and kept saying he was so sorry. So sorry for being bad. So sorry for letting everyone down. So sorry for not being good enough or perfect enough." Chief James looked down at the floor for a few moments before he continued. "He admitted to circling back on you and to making the threat. But he swore he wasn't armed. He held a stick to your back that he picked up off the ground. He asked me to apologize to you."

"He did?" Sarah was surprised.

"He did. He said he really meant no harm. He basically enacted a scene he saw in a movie to keep you from following him, from figuring out who he was. He didn't think you knew."

"He was right about that. I didn't. At least not until this morning. So what happens to him now?"

"He's a juvenile because he's not yet eighteen. So that's on his side. I talked to the district attorney off the record before I came here. I wanted to plead his case. This is Caleb's first brush with the law. He's a good kid and talented. He could get charged with two counts of arson and get probation, community service, and be sent for counseling. That would be the best case scenario."

"Do his parents know?"

"Yes. We had to notify them when we brought him in."

"Will the university rescind its offer?"

"Hard to know. Anyway, I wanted to thank you for calling this morning. It was the break we needed. And you can resume your normal life without needing to look over your shoulder or worry about being shot." The Chief grimaced as he said the words.

"Good to know," Sarah said. "I hope Caleb can straighten himself out."

The Chief was walking from the room and looked over his

shoulder. His eyes met hers. "You have a good heart, Sarah."

A small, reluctant smile flickered on her face and then a thought occurred to her. "Oh, hey Chief, Em said the Cottageville online message board mentioned the high school football coach's prize signed pigskin was stolen from his home."

"What? He didn't report it. At least I don't remember that, if he did." He spun around and faced Sarah.

"Yeah. Em said the board was lit up with speculation about why you guys pulled over Caleb this morning and someone said that maybe he was the person who broke into the house and stole the coach's football."

The Chief rushed into the grooming area. Emily was accepting money from the border collie's human companion. Chief James waited, tapping his foot, until she was through and the door had closed on the dog and its human. He looked more lively than he had when he had entered the Coiffure. "Emily, Sarah tells me there's a message online about a stolen football?" His eyebrows arched.

"Yes. There is."

"Can you show me that please?"

"Sure." Emily hit the touchpad with her thumb and her laptop screen came to life. "It's right here," she pointed at something, her index fingernail millimeters from the screen.

"Chief, the reason I brought it up," Sarah started, "is because only that one item disappeared or was stolen. That makes it sound like what happened to Ginger's necklace. I asked Em if, while she eats her lunch, she could search the message board for other posts about local thefts, especially if only one item has been taken."

"You think we might have a serial burglar?" His eyes locked on Sarah's with a piercing—yet exhausted—stare, incredulity written in every line of his face.

Sarah understood that the idea of it seemed like one thing too many today. "Don't know. I don't know any details of the coach and the football other than what Emily read. But my mind registered a possible connection."

Emily looked from the Chief to Sarah and back again. "I guess Caleb Bupp wasn't pulled over because he stole the coach's football," she said quietly.

Chief James shook his head. "It'll be everywhere soon enough. He's admitted to setting the fires."

"Holy crap on a cracker," Em said. "I didn't see that coming."

"Thank you for the information, ladies. Have a good afternoon." Chief James patted Whiskey's head one more time before he exited the Coiffure.

"OMG, Sarah. That's unreal. What about his football career? He could have made it big time."

"That may not be over." Sarah's voice was steady, hoping to calm her assistant down. "He's a juvenile and confessed. He could get probation and community service. Juvenile arrest records are sometimes sealed...or at least I think so."

"But why? Why'd he do it? He has everything going for him. Including leaving this town."

"I didn't know you didn't like it here," Sarah breathed the words out like they were painful.

"What? No. I like it here. I do. I plan to stay here. But Caleb.

Caleb has talent and the opportunity to go so many places. He can be a bigger star, a brighter star somewhere else. His talent is wasted on a town and school system this size. You know I love it here, Sarah. I do. I want to work with you forever and build and expand your business." Emily's eyes pleaded with Sarah's, as if she was asking for forgiveness for making Sarah think otherwise.

"It's okay, Em. You've been here all of your life. I'd understand if you wanted to leave, to explore outside our town, outside of our state. That's natural."

Emily shrugged. "I'd miss you and Whiskey too much."

"I appreciate that." Sarah opened her mouth to say something else but the Coiffure door opened and their next two clients walked in, trailed by the humans. It was time to get back to work.

By the end of the work day, news of Caleb's arrest had permeated all corners of Cottageville, spreading like wildfire through whispered conversations, furtive glances, and hurried text messages. The online community was ablaze with speculation, with threads unraveling on forums, social media posts commenting on every rumor, and his classmates and teachers piecing together fragments of the story in real-time.

Sarah felt a lot of sympathy for Caleb's parents, who had to have been shocked and disheartened. She wondered if they had understood their role and contribution to creating such inner turmoil in their child. Did any parent embrace that horrifying notion?

She still wondered why, of all of the possible things one could set on fire in their town, that Caleb chose the historic Christmas tree and the water tower. Did he do it to make a statement, and if so, what statement was he trying to make? Or were they the first big things his path crossed when he decided to turn something into a tiki torch? Did he have a personal or familial connection to either thing?

The questions haunted her, gnawing away at the back of her mind.

At least she could resume her solo walks and not have to waste gas and pollute the ozone by driving a mile to work and back another day. Sarah moved the load of towels from the washer to the dryer and turned it to run. Emily sat at the back table, perusing the textbook one more time, nervous energy coming off of her like waves during a sound bath. She suffered test anxiety and tonight's test was in her favorite class and she wanted to ace it.

Sarah put a hand on each of her assistant's shoulders. "You've got this. You rock. You always do." She dropped a kiss atop her head. "After your test, can you please take the towels out of the dryer and fold them?"

Emily had asked if she could take the test at the Coiffure as it was quieter than her house which was bustling with family members.

"Of course," Em replied, her head buried in her book.

"*Mi empresa es su empresa,*" Sarah improvised, hoping the meaning was clear.

Emily giggled. "You're the best. Now shoo. I have answers to give."

"Okay, okay." Sarah grabbed her jacket from the tree and put it on. She gathered her purse and keys, and picked up the boxes of prizes, and walked to the door with Whiskey on her heels. They climbed into her Jeep and drove a block and then turned right onto Main Street and then right again before the park, and then right again onto their street. Lights shone inside her house and Jared's car was still in her driveway from yesterday. The sight warmed her heart.

Mentally she noted, as she unlocked and opened her front door while holding the box under one arm, that the alarm didn't beep. She assumed Jared had turned it off. The air inside was rich with roasted chicken. It reminded her of her childhood, when Gigi had filled the house with love and delicious food and friends. She, Jared, and Whiskey really needed to entertain more often. They had such amazing friends.

"Honey, I'm home," Sarah yelled, like she was parodying Ricky Ricardo in an old episode of *I Love Lucy.*

"In the kitchen, dear," Jared yelled back, "because a man's work is never done."

"Very funny," she said, stepping into ground zero of the food prep. She wrapped her arms around him from behind as he stirred something in a pot on the stove. "Whatcha making?"

"A whole chicken is in the oven. Potatoes to mash are in the big pot. I'm sauteeing root veggies in olive oil with rosemary and sea salt."

"I love that you cook. I'm so spoiled." She kissed the side of his face. "Need help with anything?"

"Nah, you go do your usual thing. There's about thirty minutes until we eat. I'll feed Whiskey."

"Thank you, love," Sarah said, "and by the way, the arsonist was caught. He claims he meant me no harm. I'll tell you all about it over dinner."

"I heard the rumors. Caleb Bupp. What a shame."

"Yep." Sarah patted Jared's bum on her way out of the kitchen.

A few hours later, they lounged on the sofa with their bellies full, with Whiskey curled below their legs, which were stretched out on the coffee table. The dog snored softly in his sleep. A recently remade Agatha Christie movie streamed on Sarah's television, though they had already seen it. "You know," Sarah said, "since my life is no longer in danger, you don't have to stay here and protect me." She bumped Jared's socked foot with her own.

"But what if I want to. Stay here, that is?" He angled himself toward her so he could see her eyes.

"You're welcome any time."

"You've made that clear. And I'm grateful. But I've been thinking, maybe we should talk about moving in together."

"You want to talk about it or actually do it?" Sarah messed with him.

"I'd like to do it. But I figured we should talk about it, how it might change our lives. What it would or wouldn't mean. I'd like to know if it's even something you desire." He reached for her hand.

"I could get used to home cooked meals every day." Sarah's smile widened as she laced her fingers through his. "And having someone to relocate spiders for me. That's pretty appealing too."

Jared chuckled, shaking his head. "So that's what I bring to the table? Pest control and dinner?"

"Well, you're pretty good at both," she teased, leaning her head against the back of the sofa. "But seriously... I like the idea of us sharing a space. I think it could be good."

"Good?" The word had force, like he was pretending to be offended.

"Okay, great. Wonderful. Fantastic. Happy now?"

"Getting there," he said, his thumb brushing over her knuckles. "I just want to make sure this is what you want, Sarah. No pressure, no rush. I don't have to end or renew my lease until April, effective for the end of May."

"It is," she said softly, her gaze meeting his. "I don't need my life to be in danger to know I feel safe with you around. I think I'd like to feel that every day."

"Then it's settled." He grinned, his eyes sparkling. "I'll start drafting a cohabitation agreement right away."

She laughed, throwing a pillow at him. "You're such a dork."

"Your dork," he said, catching the pillow and holding it against his chest.

"Yeah," she said, a warm glow spreading through her. "My dork."

As the credits rolled on the TV, they sat there, fingers intertwined, imagining a future that felt more certain with each passing moment.

CHAPTER TWENTY

On Thursday morning when Sarah stopped by Java and Juice, Ginger was at the counter taking orders and only five tables were occupied by patrons. "Where's Jared?" Sarah asked. Whiskey waited patiently by her side for Ginger to pull out a chicken biscuit.

"He cut his finger earlier, so I sent him to urgent care to get it checked."

"How bad was it?" Sarah asked.

"Small cut but deep. I don't want him to take any chances."

"Hey, Sarah," Taylor said, rising from behind the glass display case, which he was filling with croissants, eclairs, and individually sized pies.

Sarah frowned. "Hi. Taylor." To Ginger she said, "Thank you. He didn't text me about it."

"He left like five minutes ago. He probably didn't have time." Ginger took Sarah's to-go tumbler and filled it with black dark roast coffee. "I tried a new scone recipe this morning; it's laden with toffee and dark chocolate chunks and I'm pretty sure it's calling your name."

"Of course it is. I'll take two and whatever salad you want to pawn off on me." Sarah flashed Ginger her teeth.

Ginger put two ginger and beef with cellophane noodle salads into the bag and put the scones on top. She told Sarah the total and she tapped her card. "Hey, I keep meaning to ask you. Did you get your safe installed?"

"Yes. And Daniel was so happy the guy didn't bring his son this time. When he installed the door locks, he had his teenager with him because the kid got suspended from school for fighting. So everything he did took twice as long as usual, or even longer, as he was trying to teach the kid the trade."

"Do you mean Donny Hoffmann?" Taylor interjected.

Ginger turned toward her employee. "Yeah, do you know him?"

"Isn't he a lineman on the Cottageville High football team?" Sarah asked.

"Yes and yes," Taylor said. "We play an online game together and sometimes hang out."

"Why'd he get into a fight and get suspended?" Sarah asked.

"It may have been over a girl. Someone said he's been hanging around one of the hockey player's girlfriends. Donny claims they are just friends. That he's known her for forever. But I guess the hockey player wasn't happy. He made some threats and threw the first punch. They were both suspended." Taylor shrugged, like it happened all of the time.

"So what's the name of his dad's company?" Sarah asked. "And are you happy with your safe and with his service?"

"Hoffmann Security. Paul Hoffmann is the dad. And yes, we are happy with it. Of course, pickings are slim here." Ginger's face split into a big smile.

"Noted."

"You getting a safe?"

"I might. I've been thinking about your necklace and the coach's ball and wondering if it would be prudent to lock stuff up. Even though I don't have much of value."

"It's fireproof, so good for important documents, too."

"And now you've sold me on the idea," Sarah teased.

"Glad to help."

"Come on, Whiskey, let's get to work." Sarah nodded her head in acknowledgement at some people she recognized but whose names she couldn't remember who were coming through the cafe's red door. They held it for her and Whiskey. "Thank you. Good day to you."

Sarah and Whiskey arrived at the Coiffure before Emily, so Sarah set up each station with a stack of towels, clean combs and brushes, sanitized nail trimmers, and everything they needed for their very busy day. Ten clients today had scheduled appointments, and Sarah knew they'd barely have a minute to themselves as people rushed to get their pets in spectacular style for the pet parade. She hoped there were no emergencies, like dogs who rolled in manure or cats who got covered in sap from climbing an evergreen tree, nor too many drop in nail clippings. Those things took time and that was something Sarah felt short on.

Once the Coiffure was ready for the day, Sarah remembered that Jared went to urgent care. She checked her phone. Still no message from him, so she decided to send one of her own. "Hey, Ginger said you cut yourself. Are you okay?"

She waited, but the message never went from Delivered to Read. Nor came the dots of someone responding.

Oh well, Sarah thought. *Maybe he left his phone at the cafe. He'll write when he sees the message.* She pocketed her phone in her apron, and drank her coffee, relishing the quiet while she could.

Emily arrived in her usual ensemble of black and wearing her black combat boots. Her eyes were lined with kohl and her lips were painted cherry red, which matched the heart painted on the platinum hair on the side of her head. "You're stunning today," Sarah said.

Emily blushed. "Thanks."

"Ginger tried a new scone recipe this morning."

"Awesome." Emily hung her oversized puffy coat on the tree, donned her denim dog print apron, and walked to the table in the back and set down her backpack.

"Get the results back on your test yet?" Sarah pushed a scone on a napkin toward her assistant.

"Yep." Emily took a bite of the scone and chewed. "Heaven. This is heaven."

"Well?"

"What are you? My mom?" Emily joked.

Sarah rolled her eyes.

"I got a ninety-nine percent. I missed one lousy question. Like literally missed filling in an answer. I argue that the test shouldn't have let me submit, unless every question was answered. It could have been programmed that way." Emily grimaced like an otter with indigestion.

"Ninety-nine is a stellar score. And we all make mistakes." Sarah raised her to-go tumbler. "To you, getting all A's."

Emily bumped her own tumbler into Sarah's. "I'll drink to that."

As they were bathing their first clients of the day, Sarah asked, "Hey, Em. Do you know Donny Hoffmann?"

"Yeah. I met him at Taylor's."

"What's he like?"

"Eh," Emily said. "Kind of full of himself, I think."

"What do you mean?"

"I don't know. When he was at T's, he kept saying how he could get into almost anyone's house because his dad is a locksmith and taught him the trade. I called b.s. on it. Just because his dad knows locks doesn't mean anything. Just because my dad is a doctor doesn't mean I know how to diagnose diseases. Donny kept talking and talking and he wouldn't shut it. It was like he wanted everyone to know how great he was."

"Oh, people like that annoy me."

"Me, too. Anyway, he finally shut up for a little while after one of the guys challenged him, said something like 'If you're so great with locks, how about we kick you out of Taylor's house and lock all of the doors and you see if you can get yourself back in, jackass.' Everyone there laughed, and Donny didn't say much else the rest of the night. I think they started playing a game and forgot about it."

"Huh," Sarah said, her mind moving faster than a second hand on a watch. "Em, when was this night at Taylor's when you met Donny?"

"A week ago, maybe. Oh wait, it was Friday night. The last one, the weekend of Ginger's engagement. Why?"

"Just wondering." And she was. Sarah was wondering if that exchange with his peers had given Donny Hoffmann something to prove. Could he be the one who broke into Ginger's and the coach's houses and took the necklace and the autographed football? Sarah wondered how good his lock-picking skills were, or if his dad had a master key to all of the places whose locks he installed. Did the coach have electronic locks on his house?

As she washed and groomed dog after dog, these questions tumbled through her head like puppies playing. By the time she was able to take a break to eat her salad, Sarah was surfing the internet on her computer for Coach Davis' address. He lived about seven blocks north and three blocks over, on the far side of the hospital in an area of newer built homes. It was close enough that Sarah and Whiskey could walk, but she needed to text Jared that she'd be late coming home.

She pulled out her phone from her apron and looked at the screen. She had missed a message from Jared. "Sorry. Phone was dead. Forgot to charge it last night. Finger is fine. Two stitches. Love you."

She smiled at the message. "Glad to hear you are fine. Love you too. I have to run an errand after work so Whiskey and I won't be home until six or after."

"Thanks for the heads up" was the quick reply.

Next, Sarah texted Chief James. "Did you talk to the coach about why he didn't report the stolen football?"

The answer came a few moments later. "Said he thought it was one of his players pulling a prank. They do that to each other. He figured they'd eventually cough it up."

Hmm. Sarah wasn't so sure. *Not if the two thefts are connected.*

"When did it go missing?" Sarah texted.

"A week ago, or maybe a bit longer. He wasn't exactly sure."

Sarah could see one of the players playing a prank on their coach, or even part of or the whole team for that matter. That would make sense, especially if he told them about the football or made it into a big deal. But if that same person or group of people stole Ginger's necklace, what was that about? Why was she or it a target? That was the part that didn't add up.

Sarah texted the Chief a third question: "Anyone else report missing only one valuable from their home?"

"Negative."

Sarah wondered if that was because homeowners didn't notice one of their items was gone, or if there had been only two thefts. *How many Cottageville residents had used Hoffmann Security to install locks and safes?* She used her computer to look at the company's website. It looked professional enough and stressed they had options for businesses and residences, as well as individuals needing protection, as they offered products for securing physical premises, websites and cyber information and storage, and security in the form of personal protection. They also sold top-of-the-line safes and built out safe-rooms. On the About page, the photo showed Paul Hoffmann looking very clean cut, with military-short brown hair, a thin-wale corduroy button down shirt, and piercing blue eyes. His bio said he worked in intelligence and cyber security while in the U.S. army for eight years, before moving to Cottageville and starting his own company. He was a member of the Chamber of Commerce and the Rotary club.

Sarah was curious about if the son looked like the father, so she Googled "Donny Hoffmann Cottageville" and waited to see what was found. The kid's Facebook page profile photo showed a stocky, muscled teen with longer brown hair and those same piercing blue eyes. His direct gaze into the camera read like a challenge, and Sarah felt that he looked like he had more than the proverbial chip on his shoulder; he carried a whole lumberyard. His posts were a mixture of gym and football selfies, cryptic quotes about loyalty and betrayal, and the occasional rant about people who "don't know how to mind their own business." Scrolling further, Sarah noticed a few pictures of the father and son, their body language telling its own story. Paul Hoffmann's arm rested on his son's shoulder, but Donny leaned slightly away, his expression tight. It didn't take an expert to see the tension between the two. Sarah couldn't help but speculate that some of that tension may have spilled over into Donny's interactions with others in their town.

She clicked back to Paul Hoffmann's company website and pulled out her phone to call and set up a consultation about getting a safe, but she didn't have time for that. The Coiffure's green door opened and her one o'clock client was fifteen minutes early. Whiskey ran to welcome the newcomer as Sarah forced herself to get back to work. Emily was already occupied with a black and tan Shibu Inu.

CHAPTER TWENTY-ONE

At five-twenty, Sarah and Whiskey sauntered up Main Street toward the hospital, which was ten blocks north. She hadn't been by the medical establishment since late last year and cutting through its parking lot to get to the development of newer houses on the other side brought back memories of Jared's accident and the moments she had thought she had lost him. She never wanted to feel that uncertainty and amount of anguish ever again.

"Stick close, Whiskey," Sarah commanded, as her dog jutted from taking the straight path as his nose dictated. Intriguing scents and messages were everywhere, if one was a dog.

Whiskey circled back to her side and stayed there, bringing

comfort on this cold and windy day as the sun was setting.

Twelve minutes after they had left the Coiffure, they stepped into the tract of houses. The coach's home was a two-story Colonial with a three-car garage and a postage stamp—by Iowaian standards—of a yard. And even from across the street, Sarah could see the numbered key pad on the front door and a similar system along the wall by the first of the three garage doors—just as she suspected.

That was all she needed to see so she and Whiskey made their way back across the hospital parking lot and over to Main Street, and then they cut through the park and said hello to Braidington and Coco Chanel, who were out on their evening walk. Whiskey and Coco circled three times in the sniffing dance before Sarah excused them and said they needed to be on their way, that Jared was waiting with dinner.

And he was, but not in the way Sarah was expecting. Curry punched her nostrils as soon as she opened the door. Whiskey's nose rose in the air and it wiggled and wiggled like he couldn't get enough of the delicious spice. "Hey, did you get take-out?" Sarah yelled as she removed her puffy jacket and took off her boots.

"I did. I got too busy working and left myself no time to cook. I hope you don't mind. I know you love their butter chicken."

"I do. But everything they sell is good." She met Jared in the dining room. His drawing papers, pencils, paint pens, and storyboards were spread across the table. She leaned down and kissed him where he sat. "Would you prefer to eat in the living room?"

"If you don't mind," he said. "Do you need time to shower and change?"

"Not right now. It's late and I'm hungry." Sarah met Whiskey in the kitchen where he had parked himself, staring longingly into his empty food bowl. "You're hilarious, dog. I'll feed you, though I'm sure you'd rather lick curry from the plates."

Last year when Sarah had ordered butter chicken and *palak paneer*, Whiskey had raided the kitchen trash and taken out the takeaway container and lapped every drop of curry from its insides. She was surprised he didn't get sick as spice wasn't good for dogs. Now, every time she had Indian food, he went a bit crazy, salivating, begging, and licking his lips as she ate her meal.

She nuked Whiskey's frozen raw food until it wasn't a solid block of ice as she dished basmati rice, two types of chicken, *palak paneer*, and *aloo gobi* onto two plates. She fed Whiskey and then carried the plates of food, two forks, and two napkins into the living room and motioned for Jared to sit next to her on the sofa.

He took one of the plates of food and before he put a bite into his mouth, he asked, "How was your day?"

"How was yours?" she asked, leaning over him to look at his left finger that sported a bandage.

"Good. Productive. But you didn't answer about yours." He took a bite of the chicken in its rich orangey sauce and some fluffy, fragrant rice.

"Mine was good. Busy." She ate a few bites and then eyed him, debating if she wanted to disclose what she was thinking.

He gave her the side eye and said, "What's on your mind, Sarah?"

"Umm, I have some suspicions regarding who might have taken

Ginger's necklace."

"Are your suspicions based on evidence or facts?" Jared raised one eyebrow and smirked.

"At this point I'd call it supposition though my Spidey-sense is telling me I'm on the right track."

"And we'd hate to disappoint our Spidey-sense by ignoring it." Jared's smirk turned into a full-on grin that stretched across the bottom half of his face.

"You understand me so well." Sarah kissed his grin.

"So would you like to fill me in?" Jared forked more food into his mouth.

"Yes," Sarah said, and then she launched into everything from Taylor's comments in the morning to Em's opinion of Donny Hoffmann and to her online snooping, or sleuthing as she liked to call it, and her impressions. Eventually she wound her way to her walk-by of the coach's house and the keycode locks. She ended with, "I'm thinking of setting a kind of trap, just to see what happens."

At that, Jared frowned. "What kind of trap?"

"I was thinking of either getting a safe installed or getting a second opinion on my security system."

"I see. And how would that be a trap?"

"I could leave out a valuable 'accidentally' and see if it becomes bait."

"But, Sarah, you said you suspect the son not the father. The son will most likely be in school on a weekday. He's not going to be here to see the bait."

"Well maybe his dad will mention it. As in 'this stupid lady that I saw today had diamond earrings just sitting out in the open' or something like that."

"It's not a guarantee that it would even get mentioned. It would be better if, say, Taylor told Donny about it directly and said 'you said you could get into anyone's house, try this one' but that's probably entrapment. And jewelry may or may not entice him. If everything everyone said is true, he may just be breaking in for sport and then takes something as a kind of trophy."

Sarah swallowed some food and then said, "What if when I call Paul Hoffmann I tell him that I want a second opinion on my system because both Ginger and the coach lost things of value and then ask, 'I know Ginger said you did the locks and safe at their house. Did you do the football coach's house, too?' That way he's tipped off that something shady is going on associated with his business?"

"Even if he figures it out, do you think he'll suspect his son? And even if he does, he might want to keep it quiet and they might never get their stuff back."

"Hmm," Sarah said. "This is more difficult than I imagined."

"I know," he said, putting a hand on her arm. "But you could just tell Chief James your suspicions, even with nothing concrete to go on. He seems to respect your opinion, especially since it's helped him in the past."

Sarah wrinkled her nose like she didn't like the smell of that idea. "I just hate to accuse someone without evidence. Especially someone I don't even know."

"I get that. You said that the Chief had to reach out to the coach, right, that he didn't report the theft of his ball, thought it might be a prank?"

"Yes."

"I wonder if the coach talks to the team, tells them about the theft and that now the police are involved, if Donny or whomever took the ball would suddenly make it reappear on the coach's desk or something. And if the police could stage his office beforehand with unassuming cameras to catch the culprit or culprits, then they can question them about Ginger's necklace. That's assuming the two thefts are connected."

Sarah sat up straighter and her eyes widened. "That's not a bad plan." But then she frowned, "That still means I need to tell Chief James my suspicions with no evidence to back it up."

"Not necessarily. You could present this plan under the guise of since the coach thinks it's a prank, let's use that to the police's advantage and set the stage and see if anyone acts."

"I think we just mixed some metaphors," Sarah giggled. "But I love the way your mind works. I'm gonna call the Chief."

She picked up her phone and enthusiasm cascaded from her like water from a fall as she told the police chief of one way they could possibly get the autographed football back and have a suspect to question about Ginger's necklace.

When she finished spilling the idea, she paused long enough for the Chief to say, "It's very creative. And if one of the team members took the football like the coach suspects, it could work. And if it wasn't a prank or by one of them, maybe it won't work. But it won't take too much to give it a try. Thanks for calling, Sarah."

"Thank you for listening, Chief." Sarah smiled even though he couldn't see her.

When she disconnected, Jared said, "Well done. Is there anything else we need to do tonight?"

"I need to put together the gift bags for Saturday. Why?"

"Because inspiration has struck and I'd like to go back to working on the book." Passion showed in Jared's hazel eyes.

"By all means. Go. Create. Do what you love. I'll clean up the dishes and take care of the kitchen." She leaned toward him and kissed him.

Whiskey made a squeaky growl in his throat like "Oh brother, not again."

Sarah laughed and ruffled the fur between her dog's shoulders.

After the prizes were all packaged and Sarah sent a final email to the volunteers about the time they were requested to be at their stations, an email to the vendors reminding them when and where to set up their booths, and a third email to the parade participants about where to check in and how to queue, exhaustion weighed on her. She took a shower and changed into her "Dogs Rule" pajamas and crawled into bed with a cozy mystery featuring a sleuth who could telepathically hear animals' thoughts. *What an interesting gift that would be to have,* Sarah thought. *It would come in handy with her more obstinate clients.* But the only dog she needed to fully understand was her own—and she thought they communicated flawlessly. He sighed as he used her lower leg as a pillow.

Twenty minutes into the book, Jared came into the room. "Do you plan on reading long?"

"Not sure. I'm pretty sleepy. What's up?"

"I was thinking I'd turn in. Early day tomorrow as usual." He went into the bathroom to prepare for bed.

When he slid between the covers Sarah asked, "Does your finger hurt? The one that you sliced?"

"It burns a little. But fortunately I'm right handed."

"How did you cut it?"

"Big knife, big carrot. My fingers were too close to the knife. The usual way people cut themselves." He flashed her a smile that reached his eyes.

"I'm glad you're okay and that you didn't cut your finger off."

"Nope. But I did almost hit the bone."

"Ouch. That's deep."

"Eh. Fingers are thin. Not much fat padding." He interlaced his left fingers, including the bandaged one, with her right fingers. "Good night, mi'lady. And good night, fair canine."

"Good night, my lord. Sleep well." She pressed her lips against his for a split second, and then closed her book and placed it on her nightstand. She double checked that her phone was plugged in. That's when she noticed a text from the Chief. It said, "Coach said game on."

A smile graced Sarah's face and she settled into her side of the bed and closed her eyes to welcome her dreams.

CHAPTER TWENTY-TWO

By Friday afternoon, the whole town was rippling from the shocks of the arrest of a second and third high schooler within the space of a few days. This was something the town had never seen. The coach, in a before-school mandatory meeting, played his part well, yelling his disappointment in how a stupid prank had gotten out of control and sent the police to his doorstep, embarrassing him in front of his neighbors and his friends. Somehow, somewhere, a video of the meeting had leaked to the internet.

Sarah and Emily watched it, mouths agape at what they saw. "I have a well-respected position in this community," the coach said, "and I can't afford to have the Chief of Police show up at my door in broad daylight. Things like that create scandal, and rumors run rampant in a small town like ours. Did you think, did you think about that when you planned to steal my autographed football as a prank? Did you think I wouldn't notice or care? Of course I do. And I didn't report it because I thought you guys thought it was funny. That eventually you'd cough it up and we'd have a good laugh, like we have in the past. Like when you all went to dump the water from the sports cooler over Caleb's head when we beat the lions, but I had secretly dyed the water blue. Man, it took a few days until you were all scrubbed clean." The coach laughed and titters made their way around the room.

"But this, this isn't funny. Not when the police come a-calling. Not when they come to question me in my home in front of my wife and kids. That just makes me angry and disgusted and embarrassed and let down. After everything I do for you kids." He shook his head and hung it like he felt shame.

The players—Caleb with them, as he was out on bail—seemed afraid to make eye contact with the coach or any of their teammates. As they sat on the floor of the gym, their eyes slid from side to side and up and down like the silver ball in a pinball machine, wanting to be everywhere and nowhere at once.

The coach continued, "If one of you knuckleheads took my ball in a prank that has gone awry, you have two hours to put it back on my desk. I will ask you no questions nor will I ruin your life." He emitted a deep, menacing laugh.

Sarah could feel the tension charge like an electric bug zapper through the football team. Some of them had their hands clasped together and their knuckles were turning white.

"Two hours," the coach reiterated, before he stormed out of the gym.

As soon as he cleared the room, the boys jumped into action. Caleb stepped into his role of team captain and demanded the perpetrator, "Fix this shit. I've got enough problems without dealing with this," he said.

Snide smiles could be seen on some of his teammates' faces.

"Who took it?" a boy Sarah didn't know asked the group.

No one answered his question. They murmured amongst themselves before dispersing as a bell rang.

The video ended there.

"Wow, Sarah. That was intense. I wonder who made this video." The uploader's user handle was CTVLE999.

"No idea."

Before the video had appeared online, a poster on the message board wrote, "Police picked up Donny Hoffmann and Craig Pierce." Speculation rang out like gunshots in the comments with guesses including drugs, indecent exposure, fighting, and breaking into the principal's office and changing grades.

But then when the video was uploaded, people drew new, more accurate conclusions.

Some people thought it was much ado about nothing. Others wrote, "That's theft not a prank." A few people questioned why youth today were so much less respectful than they were back in the day.

Emily commented, "Like our parents and grandparents never pulled a prank. The stuff they've shared with me is way worse than this. My grandpa says he used to pour ketchup on his arm, climb into the trunk of the car with his arm hanging out, and have his buddy drive him around town, like he had a dead body barely hidden."

"Wow. That's rich. And what an image," Sarah said. "I wonder if Donny and Craig have Ginger's necklace or if that's been recovered."

"I figure we'll hear about it eventually," Emily said, as she led their latest client into the wash tub. The French spaniel was calm and docile and followed Emily's lead like a dog who lived to please.

Sarah's phone chimed in a text. Chief James said, "I'm stopping by EOD."

"To the Coiffure?" she responded.

"Yes."

"Okay."

Sarah washed and groomed an American Eskimo dog, and when she was done, the dog was so fluffy and full and his fur so white Em joked he'd give his human snow blindness. And then for their last dog of the day, Emily and Sarah tag-teamed a beautiful Black Russian Terrier that weighed one hundred and thirty pounds. Onyx's breed had served in military operations for decades, but the massive dog in their wash tub had a love-filled heart and a gentle disposition that made her a great companion for the elementary-school aged kids in her household. Onyx, along with her humans, younger and older, would be marching in tomorrow's parade. When they finished with her spa treatment, Sarah tied a royal purple and hot pink heart bandana around her neck, which she seemed to wear proudly, stretching her neck a bit taller.

Emily handled the handing over pets to their people and collecting payment for services rendered while Whiskey supervised, and Sarah started the laundry, swept the floor, and scrubbed their work areas. She was tired and thankful the Coiffure was closed for the next two days. She had kept her calendar clear on Sunday to give herself time for self-care and recovery.

Just as Em was removing her apron, putting on her coat, and saying goodbye, Chief James opened the green door. "Emily. Sarah. Whiskey," he said, nodding his head to each of them.

Emily hesitated in her departure.

"It's okay, Em. I'll see you tomorrow at seven-thirty."

"Okay," Emily said, then behind the Chief's back she held her hand to the side of her head, with her pointer, middle, and index fingers bent, her pinky at her mouth, and her thumb near her ear in the universal sign for "Call me."

Sarah winked in acknowledgement.

The bags under the Chief's eyes looked more like roller boards and his hair was once again in disarray around his cap.

"You've had a rough week," Sarah said.

"I'll be glad when it's over." Chief James rubbed his hand over his face before he looked Sarah in the eyes. "Did you know it was Donny Hoffmann who took the football and Ginger's necklace?"

"I didn't know." Sarah stressed the word 'know.' "But I had suspicions. I had no evidence or knowledge. I didn't even have hearsay."

"What made you suspicious?"

Sarah explained how Ginger and Daniel had hired Hoffmann Security to install their locks and their safe, but how they hadn't gotten around to installing security cameras, and how Paul had brought his suspended-from-school son with him the day he installed the locks.

She shared her knowledge that the only way through the doors was to use a master key thingy or to know the code. From there, she told him about Taylor's offhand comment and Emily's repeating of Donny's boast and Emily's character assessment of the teen. She admitted to cyber-sleuthing for a photo and Donny's online posts. And how she felt sure that the stealing of only one thing seemed more like for sport or something to prove than an actual theft—by a professional or someone wanting quick-sale things to score drugs.

Sarah said she mentally questioned if the coach had also had the same type of keycode locks installed by Hoffmann Security. And when she thought about why only Ginger and the coach seemed to have things taken didn't make sense unless it was only because it was a crime of opportunity. "I'm not sure what the boy told you," Sarah said, "but my guess is he went to Ginger's because he knew he could get in, that he had no foreknowledge of the necklace but took it because it was one of the things he saw that was clearly of value."

"I'm amazed at how you pieced this together, Sarah. And how you set it up or planted the seed with us of a potential plan to catch the thief without making an accusation against someone, especially when none of us had proof. That was rather brilliant."

Sarah chuckled and felt her face blush. "Thank you."

"Donny admitted he took the football to both play a prank and because he was sick and tired of the coach talking about his signed football. He also wanted to impress his friends. He had running back Pierce with him when he broke into the coach's house."

"Wow. That's trust, that Pierce would keep his mouth shut."

Chief James nodded. "Yes. Young and dumb. When we brought

them in, Pierce sang quicker than the proverbial canary. But he had no knowledge of Ginger's necklace. Only Donny knew what I was talking about. I could see it in his eyes. And it didn't take long until he admitted it. Said he broke in and took it to prove he could." The Chief grimaced. "He really is a bit full of himself. Emily is right. But he gave up the necklace quickly. He had the box wrapped in a towel and shoved into the back of his school locker. I returned it to her an hour ago, after we processed and photographed it."

"Oh, I'm so happy to hear it has been returned. But what is going to happen to the boys?"

"I don't know for sure. The coach isn't pressing charges for the theft of the football, but he asked me if he could force those two players to do some extra dirty community service." His face broke into a grin, bringing some light to his tired eyes.

"And the necklace?"

"It's worth a lot more so that will be up to the District Attorney, but once again, both Donny and Craig are underage. Hell, Donny should be grateful we arrested him today. Tomorrow is his eighteenth birthday."

"Oh my."

"Anyway, since the idea was yours, or yours and Jared's, I wanted you to know the truth about what happened and to thank you for your help. And once again I'm extending the offer, if you ever get tired of grooming dogs, I'll make a place for you on my team. You have a mind for mystery and I'm glad you share it with us." He extended his hand.

Sarah extended hers and they shook. "Thank you."

Whiskey, who was lying on his side on the sofa this whole time, let loose a single "Woof."

A few moments later as they walked home, Sarah felt an inner glow of jobs well done. She and Emily had gotten through what seemed like a never-ending stream of animals the last couple of weeks. She had survived a threat on hers and Whiskey's lives and now had a house with top-notch security to keep her safe through any number of potential problems. She grew closer with her friends and neighbors and with Jared. And she had helped solve two new mysteries that plagued people she cared about. Life was good. Now all she had to do was ensure the Valentine's Day Pet Parade and related activities were fun and well-run for everyone.

CHAPTER TWENTY-THREE

The crisp winter morning of Cottageville's inaugural Valentine's Day Pet Parade dawned with the sun peeking over the horizon, casting long shadows across the town's snow-dusted streets. Sarah Carter stood in front of a closed storefront on Main Street taking in the sights. The street was now lined with colorful booths and banners in shades of pink and red. The air was sharp, the sky a brilliant shade of blue, and despite the frosty temperatures, the small town was buzzing with excitement.

"Here we go," Sarah muttered to herself, pulling her scarf tighter around her neck. Her auburn hair was tucked beneath a cozy knit beanie, but even that couldn't entirely protect her from the mid-

February chill. Beside her, Whiskey trotted back and forth, his tail wagging in anticipation, as if he knew something big was about to happen.

"Alright, Whisk. This is it," Sarah said, smiling down at her dog. "It's our big day."

She could hear the faint hum of activity from the other end of the street. Volunteers from the Grange Hall had set up barricades and signs, directing the pet parade participants to their designated areas. Over the past couple of weeks, Sarah had gone from excitement to overwhelming anxiety and back again, but now that the day was here, the feeling was almost electric. Despite all her nerves, the sheer joy of seeing so many pet lovers together made it all worth it.

The town was ready.

Her thoughts were interrupted by the sound of familiar voices approaching. From behind her, Emily approached up with a clipboard in hand, dressed warmly in an ankle length black coat and black knit hat. "Sarah, we're almost there. The floats are lining up now, and I've ensured everyone understands that the route is up Main Street and then through the park, stopping at the make-shift stage. We just need to make sure everyone checks in."

"Great," Sarah replied, exhaling a breath she didn't realize she was holding. "I can't believe it's finally here."

"Hey, it'll be fine. You've got this," Emily reassured her, glancing down at Whiskey, who was alert to all of the activity of people and their pets in costume. "Whiskey's just here for the treats, huh?"

"Pretty much," Sarah said, laughing. "I told him he's walking down the street in style today, even if he doesn't wear a costume. A red velvet bow tie will have to do."

Emily grinned. "Debonair. Classic. I'd expect nothing less from the handsome boy." She wiggled her fingers under his chin and Whiskey gave her a black gummed grin in response.

Sarah's phone buzzed in her pocket, and she pulled it out quickly to check the message. It was from Bill, who had been a huge help with organizing the volunteers. He had emailed over the finalized list of volunteers that had shown up for the day. Sarah quickly skimmed through it, her eyes landing on names like Janice Jenkins, who was manning the check-in table, and Bill himself, who had volunteered to coordinate traffic and security. She really needed to do something extra special for them for all of their help.

Feeling a small sense of relief, Sarah looked up to see the first of the parade participants arriving—Petunia the descented skunk from Cottageville Animal Rescue, of all things, strutted down the street in a pink heart-themed outfit. "Well, this should be interesting," Sarah muttered under her breath, feeling a surge of nervousness. Whiskey had already shown signs of suspicion around Petunia during their last meeting at the park, and Sarah couldn't help but wonder if the parade would become a chaotic scene with so many different species.

"Here we go, Sarah. Let's get this show on the road!" Bill called out, hurrying toward her with his gray hair peeking out from under a worn trapper's hat.

"Thanks again for all your help, Bill," Sarah said as he approached. "I honestly don't know how I would have managed without you."

"You're welcome. You just focus on keeping things running smoothly. We've got this." Bill grinned and patted Whiskey's head.

"That dog is ready to be the star of the show."

Whiskey emphasized Bill's comment with a sharp bark of agreement, which caused Sarah, Bill, and Emily to laugh.

"He's a character, but I'm not sure he's a star," Sarah said.

As the clock ticked closer to parade time, Sarah and Emily took their positions at the check-in table, directing participants to their designated spots along the route. The dogs, cats, and various other animals—including a snake in a sequined jacket and a rabbit wearing heart-shaped sunglasses—began to assemble. There was a palpable sense of excitement in the air, as families and pet owners chatted with each other, checking on their animals and making last-minute costume adjustments.

"Alright, you're up next," Emily said, waving to Sarah. The first group of pet participants was beginning to line up at the starting point. "Everything's good to go on this end."

"I'll be right there," Sarah replied, her eyes scanning the crowd as the parade participants began to move.

Bill had been right: the volunteers were doing an excellent job coordinating the foot traffic and keeping everyone organized. There were no signs of trouble—yet. Sarah took one more deep breath, feeling her anxiety begin to ease.

As the parade began to march up Main Street, Sarah felt her heart swell with pride. She was overwhelmed by the sheer joy on display—this wasn't just a parade, it was a celebration of community. People were everywhere, cheering on their furry—and scaly—friends as they strutted down the street in their finest Valentine's Day attire.

Iggy the iguana crawled along in his red heart-patterned sweater, his handler, Taylor, grinning proudly beside him. The crowd cheered as Iggy, surprisingly unfazed by the cold, made his way past the spectators, his tiny claws clicking against the pavement.

Next came the poodles, Kahlo and Cassatt, who were both dressed to the nines in the outfits Gladys had described. Kahlo sported a cute beret and a red heart sweater, while Cassatt wore a headpiece that looked like a kissing booth, complete with a small sign reading "Kiss Me for a Treat!" The crowd laughed and clapped, and the poodles pranced down the street, tails wagging proudly as their owner, Gladys, waved and threw kisses to the crowd from behind them.

Sarah's heart warmed. She wished Gigi was alive to see her best friend shine behind her poodles. It was moments like this that made all the stress worthwhile.

A dozen parade participants later came the real test: Petunia the skunk, walking proudly in her pink bow and Valentine's Day dress. Whiskey, who had been observing from the sidelines, let out a low growl as she came closer. Sarah winced, but to her relief, Petunia calmly passed by without incident. The crowd oohed and aahed, clearly impressed by her cuteness—and Sarah breathed a sigh of relief.

As the parade continued, Sarah couldn't help but smile as more and more animals took their turn down Main Street: the fluffy golden retriever in a heart-patterned cape, the Chihuahua dressed as Cupid, and even a hamster wearing a tiny tutu, held gently in its young owner's mittened hands as she marched proudly behind her neighbors and friends.

Before long, Sarah's stress melted away completely. Everything was going smoothly—better than expected, even. The volunteers had stepped up and made Sarah's job easier. The animals were happy and calm (for the most part), and the crowd's energy was contagious. It felt like the whole town had come together to celebrate, and Sarah couldn't be prouder of what she and Emily had created.

Sarah, Emily, and Whiskey walked after the last of the parade participants, and Sarah encouraged the spectators to join them on their walk to the park. More fun and festivities awaited them there at the small stage in Cottageville Park, which had been set up for the costume contest. The stage was near the burnt-out tree and next to Mayor Trish's hug-a-tree fundraising booth.

Sarah couldn't help but laugh as the various pet participants took their turns showing off their costumes for the judges, Jared Greene, Carol Binds, and Janice Jenkins. Petunia the skunk won first place in the "Most Creative Costume" category, while Iggy the iguana took home "Best in Show" for his dedication to the Valentine's theme. The prizes were ribbons, bragging rights, and the swag bags Sarah had put together on Thursday night.

After the judging wrapped up, Sarah made her way through the crowd, thanking volunteers, pet owners, and vendors for their help. Mayor Trish said at last count, they had raised more than two thousand dollars for a new tree. Sarah's heart swelled with gratitude—this small-town Valentine's Day Pet Parade and related festivities had exceeded her wildest expectations.

Later that evening, as she sat at home sipping hot chocolate curled up with her legs under her on her sofa, Whiskey napping next to her hip, and with Jared on her other side, Sarah couldn't stop smiling. The parade had been a success, and more importantly, it had brought the town closer together in a way she hadn't anticipated. Mayor Trish had loved it so much, she said she would sign an executive order to make it an annual event. "I think we did it," Sarah said, smiling at Jared, who had been there to cheer her on and to work the Java and Juice booth all day.

Jared grinned back. "I knew you would. And I'd say this calls for a celebration."

"It definitely does," Sarah agreed, raising her mug in a toast. "To Cottageville—and to the best parade ever."

And as they clinked mugs, Sarah realized that, despite the madness and the stress, she wouldn't have traded this day or the last couple of weeks for anything.

"I meant more than celebrating with hot chocolate, Sarah. Today marks our first February fourteenth as a couple."

"Oh." Sarah chuckled. "Want me to break open some bubbly?" She started to stand, but Jared's hand on her arm pulled her back down.

"Unnecessary. I want to give you your gift. Stay right there."

Jared stood and left the living room.

Sarah's heart raced like a hummingbird in anticipation.

When he returned it was with a bigger gift than Sarah imagined. Red tissue paper covered a twenty by twenty-four inch rectangle. Joy and expectation filled Sarah as her fingers found and opened the tape holding the paper together.

"Just rip it open," Jared said. "It's okay to act like a child or animal." He grinned at her.

"Oh okay." Sarah had a surge of exhilaration as she tore through the paper and it landed on the floor.

She was face to face with herself, except in superhero form, in a tight green unitard with a flat stomach, and slightly bigger boobs than she possessed, a white cape flying behind her, gold boots on her feet, and a superhero red heeler cattle dog grinning by her side. "I love it!" Tears of happiness filled her eyes. "You really see me like this?"

Jared wrapped his arms around her and pulled her to him. "I do and so does everyone who knows you. I love you, Sarah."

"I love you, too. But now my gift to you feels kinda lame." Sarah set the original framed artwork on the coffee table and padded into her bedroom. Hidden in the back of her closet was Jared's gift. It, too, was large—even larger than Jared's gift as this was more than forty-five inches across—and rectangular. It was wrapped in construction paper hearts that she cut herself and wrote sayings on in red marker, reminiscent of old-school candy hearts.

Jared opened his gift to find a super bright ultra-thin LED light box. "Wow."

"I thought you could use more light from underneath while working on your drawings."

"I could and this one is one of the best of its kind. It's also pricey. Thank you. Thank you so much."

"I was going to say it isn't really romantic...but now that you gave me a Jared original, it may be more full of love than I expected." Sarah giggled. "And Jared, I've thought some more about us and our relationship. I'd like you to move in when your lease is up. I talked it over with Whiskey and he offered his paw of approval."

"All right, Whiskey, give me five," Jared said, slapping his hand to the dog's front paw, as the dog was too tired and lazy to move from Sarah's side.

"He'll be more excited when you officially move in. And we could clear out that third bedroom and turn it into your studio."

Jared's eyes widened in surprise. "I'd love that." He wrapped Sarah in his arms and when he lowered his head to kiss her, she felt the promise of a fabulous, love-filled future in that kiss. It was a Valentine's Day she wouldn't forget.

The End

223

Want more Whiskey the Cattle Dog Mysteries? Read a sneak preview of book five in the series, *Felonies and Fireworks*, which will be released on June 1. To sign up to receive sneak previews and release dates about other books in the Whiskey Dog Mystery Series, go to https://www.whiskeydogmysteries.com

FELONIES
AND
FIREWORKS

WHISKEY DOG MYSTERY #5

CHAPTER 1

Red-haired Sarah Carter was grateful for a rare day off from Carter's Canine Coiffure, her dog grooming business in Cottageville, Iowa. So far, the year had been a whirlwind. February kicked off with the first annual Valentine's Day Pet Parade and related festivities, an idea Sarah and her assistant, Emily Holt, came up with after binge-watching too many dog videos on social media. During that same time, Sarah had helped the police solve two crimes: an arson case and the disappearance of an heirloom necklace and the high school football coach's prized autographed football.

March brought another kind of excitement, a less dangerous kind, when Sarah's parents flew in from Seattle for a couple week visit. It was especially awesome since she hadn't seen them in almost a year.

From late March through April, Sarah supported her

boyfriend, Jared Greene, as he took a break from his full-time job at Java and Juice so he could zig-zag around the country on a media tour promoting his graphic novel, which was released in April to critical acclaim. At the end of April, during a brief pause in his tour, Jared gave up his apartment above a garage and moved in with Sarah and her Australian red heeler cattle dog, Whiskey, into the Craftsman bungalow she had inherited from her grandmother, Gigi, about seven years earlier.

Since moving in, Jared had been juggling multiple responsibilities: his shifts at the cafe, owned by Sarah's best friend Ginger Jones, unpacking and unboxing his life, fulfilling his book promotion commitments, and working on his next graphic novel, which was due to his New York City publisher in the fall. Jared's rising popularity had kept him busy with podcast interviews, both morning and late show appearances, and some bookstore events on both coasts and in one of his favorite places, Chicago.

When Jared first moved to Cottageville after university, he chose the town for its affordable, art-filled community, where he could further his passions and eventually reach his goals of becoming an illustrator and author. Now, with some of his aspirations accomplished— including an invitation to give a keynote address at Comic-Con in San Diego—Sarah saw the toll that constant demands had taken on him and felt his exhaustion.

Today, while Jared worked at the cafe to make up for some of the hours he had been off, Sarah decided to surprise him by transforming her cluttered third bedroom into a suitable studio for Jared. She planned to install a reclaimed wood and wrought iron tiltable drafting table under the big backyard facing windows, so Jared had plenty of natural light for his artwork. Her best friend fiance Daniel Snyder, owner of Buck and Son hardware, was scheduled to deliver the table any minute.

But first, Sarah had to deal with Whiskey, who was outside in a staring death match with Mozart, the patched tabby belonging to Robert Wise, their neighbor from two doors up.

"Whiskey," Sarah yelled, "Mozart doesn't want to be herded. It's a cat thing. That's why he's hissing and arching his back. Leave the poor cat alone, boy."

Whiskey's rust-colored ears turned like they were satellites searching for signals. But he kept his eyes on the feline with its fur bristling along its spine like a wave frozen in time. Its narrowed eyes glinted with sharp intensity, a piercing gaze that seemed to warn against any approach. Ears flattened against its head, its tail lashed back and forth with a rhythm nothing like its namesake but that betrayed its tension.

And yet Whiskey wouldn't take the hint. He wanted Mozart to play with him and to like him. But time and again Mozart preferred to sit on their fence and taunt the dog rather than run, chase, or wrestle, like Whiskey did with his canine companions. Disdain oozed from the cat once he confirmed Whiskey couldn't reach him. He licked his arm leisurely while side-eying the dog.

Finally, Sarah had had enough. She marched into the side yard and grabbed her dog by his collar. "Come on, Whisk. We don't have all day."

That was a bit of a lie, since in truth, they did have all day. This

Saturday in late June they had nothing on their schedule—except cleaning the house and setting up Jared's studio—until the evening. And at the moment, it was only ten a.m.

Just as Sarah coaxed Whiskey inside, he bolted to the front door, barking like marauders were storming the front yard. Sarah spied the Buck and Son delivery truck in her driveway so she opened the door wide. Whiskey took that as an invitation to greet his friend, Daniel, which he did with the exuberance of a sea otter with a sea urchin, licking his hand and closing his mouth around it and pulling like he was welcoming Daniel into their home.

Daniel laughed. "Give me a minute, bud, I have work to do."

Whiskey thumped his tail on the ground in anticipation.

Daniel's assistant stepped down from the passenger side of the truck. He was built like he wrestled professionally and maybe took steroids, and he introduced himself as Tiny Tim. Sarah's eyes widened in response to his name; she shook his proffered hand. Whiskey sat at Tim's feet and offered his own hand to the man, who leaned over and shook Whiskey's paw. "You have the coolest dog."

Sarah chuckled. "He certainly thinks so."

The men went around to the back of the truck, installed a metal ramp to the tailgate, and slid a dolly under the big crate. Tim tilted the crate toward himself on the dolly and walked it backwards down the ramp while Daniel spotted and called out directions and things to avoid. When they got to Sarah's small porch, Daniel placed a sturdy sheet of wood over her steps and he and Tim slowly guided the crate and dolly up the plywood and through her front door.

"Through the living room and down the short hallway and on

the right," Sarah said, though she knew Daniel knew her house well since they were good friends.

Once they narrowly fit the crate through the bedroom door, Daniel asked Sarah where she wanted the desk. She pointed to the wall where the big windows were. "I figured it should be centered under the windows."

"Okay."

Tim removed a crowbar from his back pocket, and the crowbar bit into the narrow gap between the crate's lid and its sturdy frame, the metal scraping against wood with a grating screech. With a firm grip and a grunt of effort, Tim leveraged the tool downward, forcing the lid to creak and groan under the pressure. The wood resisted stubbornly at first, the nails holding fast like teeth clenched against intrusion. But with a sharp crack, the seal broke, and the lid splintered upward, revealing white foam sheeting protecting the metal and wood within.

With much noise, that sent Whiskey running from the room, Tim removed the sides from the crate and then he and Daniel lifted the table to the space Sarah had indicated. They let her cut cautiously through the foam with a box cutter until the beauty of the old reclaimed wood and the charcoal of the metal gleamed in a ray of light through the window.

"That's some table," Tim said.

"Sarah's boyfriend is Jared Greene, the artist,' Daniel explained.

"Ahh, that barista-turned-big-shot?" Tim nodded his head like he was impressed.

Sarah grinned at Daniel, feeling proud that people knew Jared's name.

"Need anything else?" Daniel asked Sarah.

"No. I'm good."

"Okay then. We'll get this packing and the crate parts out of your way and we'll be on our way. You may want to run a shop vac in here before Whiskey visits this room. There could be splinters."

"Good thinking," Sarah said. While the guys cleaned up the mess, she popped into her garage to get the cylindrical vacuum that had been in residence since her grandparents had lived in the house.

Sarah and Whiskey walked the men to their Buck and Son truck. Sarah shook Tiny Tim's massive hand once again and gave Daniel a hug and thanked them. And then she returned to the now-studio and shut Whiskey out of the room while she ran the shop vac. Then she set up the daylight lamp and stand so Jared would have plenty of light, installed his big wooden standing easel in a corner, also near the window, and moved the boxes he had stashed in the garage marked "STUDIO" into the space.

Sarah didn't want to overstep by opening any of the boxes so she left them for him to unpack and put away. At least the space now felt welcoming for work.

The rest of the time, until Jared came home at three, Sarah used to clean the two and a half bathrooms and the kitchen, to vacuum the rugs and mop the hardwoods, and to prepare a picnic for their supper. Tonight, they planned to attend the community movie at Cottageville Park.

Four hours later, Whiskey, off-leash as usual, Sarah, and Jared walked up their street and looked both ways before venturing over the cross-street and into the park. Sarah scanned the people in the park, as they planned to sit with three early-octogenarian friends: Gladys Rossmiller, who had been Gigi's best friend; Sarah's across the street neighbor Mrs. Janice Jenkins, who was now Gladys' closest friend; and Bill Reid, a widower whose company was sought after by Cottageville's gray-haired granny set and who seemed to be close to or dating both Gladys and Janice. Sarah carried a tote bag with bug spray; Whiskey's water and food; a big blue, black, and white Mexican blanket; and hers and Jared's sweatshirts in case it got chilly after the sun completely set. They were both currently in shorts and t-shirts. Jared carried the wicker picnic basket with their food, plates, and utensils, as well as a bottle of wine and plastic stemware since glass wasn't permitted within the park.

Sarah spied Gladys in a pastel tracksuit and her two miniature poodles, Kahlo and Cassatt, with Bill a few yards away, so she walked in that direction, but of course, Whiskey beat her to the destination. He sniffed his friends and slurped Kahlo's ear with his big tongue. Bill, wearing jeans and a faded gray t-shirt, opened one lawn chair and then another and then a third, placing each in the grass facing the screen that looked wider and taller than Sarah's house.

"Take a seat, Glad." He motioned to the chairs and Gladys chose the one on the right. "Sarah, why don't you put your blanket in front of us and we'll put our cooler on your blanket, if you don't mind."

"That's fine by me," Sarah said. Once she and Jared had the blanket spread and all of their things laid out on top of it, she officially greeted Gladys and Bill with hugs and scratched under the poodles' chins.

Whiskey wandered nearby saying hello to Sascha the German shepherd and to Police Chief James Order and his wife Barbara and to some of his other friends.

Wearing pull-on linen pants and a lilac button-down shirt, Janice arrived with a tote filled with delicious delicacies and lowered herself into the left hand chair next to Bill, just as Mayor Trish McGowan spoke into the microphone. "Thank you, friends and neighbors, for coming for tonight's film. We offer the free Saturday night films and the Sunday evening concerts all summer long to foster a sense of community and to help you get to know one another. Tonight's film is the family-friendly Inside Out, a little over an hour and a half animated emotional rollercoaster that may have you laughing and crying in the same few seconds." Trish smiled. "And now on with the show."

Sarah asked Whiskey to return to their blanket and sit, which he did after lapping up some water. She placed his food bowl in front of him and he gobbled it down like he was in a world-record setting eating contest. "Slow down, Whisk," Sarah admonished. "Don't make yourself sick."

His brown eyes met her green ones like he had no idea what she was talking about. She shook her head and petted his neck. He laid down and cuddled against her leg.

Jared handed Sarah a plate of perfect picnic food: potato salad, baked beans, and chicken salad with celery and dried cranberries, of all of which Sarah made fresh earlier in the day. He also handed her a glass of Sauv Blanc, and quietly asked Bill, Gladys, and Janice if they would like anything. In unison, the three stopped chewing, gave Jared a smile, and politely responded, "No, thank you." They were enjoying smoked turkey and havarti sandwiches and a fruit salad Janice had made.

The movie started and Sarah was mesmerized by both the vibrant colors of the characters on screen as well as how relatable the story was. She had seen the movie before, when it first came out, but as it played before her, she realized how much of it she didn't remember...and why it had won an Academy Award. The storyline, the voice over acting, and the animation were all so engaging and well-done.

Thirty or forty mesmerizing minutes into the film, Whiskey's eyes popped open and he wriggled his nose like he caught a scent. He released a whimper, which set Sarah on edge. "What is it?" she whispered to him. He popped up onto all fours and turned around staring at Bill, who suddenly grabbed his chest and opened his mouth, eyes bugging behind his glasses in fear.

Sarah's heart beat staccato in her chest. "Call nine-one-one," Sarah said aloud to Jared. "Bill's having a heart attack."

Sign up to follow Faith Walker and to never miss another Whiskey Dog Mystery release. Go to http://www.whiskeydogmysteries.com or follow us on social media @whiskeydogmysteries.